PIRATING THE ALIEN

BEASTLY ALIEN BOSS, BOOK 7

AVA ROSS

FOREWORD

A note to the reader.

If you found this book outside of Amazon,
it's likely a stolen/pirated copy.
Authors make nothing when books are pirated.
If authors are not paid for their work,
they can't afford to keep writing.

*For my parents who
always believed I could do this.*

SERIES BY AVA

Mail-Order Brides of Crakair

Brides of Driegon

Fated Mates of the Ferlaern Warriors

Fated Mates of the Xilan Warriors

Holiday with a Cu'zod Warrior

Galaxy Games

Alien Warrior Abandoned

Beastly Alien Boss

Bride of the Fae

A Sci-Fi Holiday Tail

Monsterville, USA

Monster on Board
(co-written with Alana Khan)

You can find her books on Amazon.

PIRATING THE ALIEN

I'm falling for my space pirate boss, but rogue aliens are after him—and now me.

It was a simple job. Sneak aboard a pirate spaceship and steal a precious artifact from the brooding, too-hot captain, Matis. Before I know it, I'll be on my way back to Earth with enough credits to cure my mom's sickness.

Is it my fault I accidentally stab him? Instead of making me walk the interstellar plank, he makes me serve as his cabin boy. Good thing he doesn't realize I'm not a boy.

His snarly outside hides a squishy center, but someone's out to kill him, and who needs to get tangled up in that? Then we're trapped on a rogue space station with alien pirates trying to kill us.

He discovers my secret.

He says we'll escape—and then he's claiming me as his fated mate.

Pirating the Alien is Book 7 of the Beastly Alien Boss Series. Each book is standalone and only loosely connected. They can be read in any order. Expect strong women and heroes who are battle-ready, who talk dirty, and who will do everything to be with their fated mates.

CHAPTER ONE
TATUM

When you wake each morning to your mom hacking her lungs out, and the doctors tell you her terminal genetic malformation can be easily cured with a sizeable amount of credits, you'll lie, steal, and maybe even kill to get that cure.

My regular job paid me a decent wage, but it would never be enough for a bill like that. Mom had been sick a very long time. I couldn't stand by and watch her die, not when I could do something about it.

I went to the Interstellar Employment Agency to find a better-paying job, and they gave me three offers. I wasn't interested in being a nanny to two hellion alien younglings, and the thought of massaging the legs of a hundred-legged Vellicore twice a day didn't hold much appeal. But the mystery of the third job intrigued me. That and the huge salary I'd be paid for a short period of time.

Leaving Mom with all the credits I had and enough

medicine for almost a full lunar cycle, I promised to return to her as soon as I could. I was transported to the Plushier Space Station, where I was directed by my wrist com to a secluded location to meet up with my new boss.

The Ergeepelon alien wasn't one for chatting. He laid it out the second I introduced myself.

"You need sneak onto spaceship," he said in choppy universal language. Shifting his six limbs, he kept his face in shadows. His segmented exoskeleton scraped and ground against his other body parts, and the taint of rotting flesh drifted off his shell, hitting my sinuses like I'd stuffed garbage up there.

"That's it? Sneak on board a spaceship?" I panted through my mouth, but I could almost *taste* him. "How am I supposed to do that?"

"We send you in supply capsule. Bots on Skaros Space Station pull you in. When hatch open, you climb out. Seek this ship." He tapped my wrist com—the one they'd sent when I was hired—with a spiked claw, and a name appeared.

"Snuggles?" I asked in amazement. "Who in the galaxy names a starship something like that?"

"Captain."

I shrugged; it hardly mattered what the ship was called.

"Recommend not let them see you," the Ergeepelon lisped, tilting his long, triangular head, watching me with his three black eyes. "They pirates. Slit throat."

I'd take a pass on that.

"Isn't Skaros a floating pile of space junk?" I wasn't

sure about this assignment. There was something he wasn't telling me. "Last I heard, they were having gravity and oxygen problems."

A growl ripped through his segmented body. "They fix all problems." He poked my chest with both of his front limbs, the spikes causing pain even if they didn't break the skin. I'd irritated him. The thought of angering him made my heart seize. "Once on board, find safe in main stateroom, steal artifact."

"What kind of artifact?"

My new com flashed the image of a stone statue about the height and width of my forearm depicting an alien lady in a long flowing gown, her pleading gaze pointed toward the heavens. "Why is this so valuable to you?"

"No question. Want credits? Do job."

The job didn't sound too challenging, and I did need the credits. "Once I have the statue in my position, how will I get it to you?"

"Tap com. We extract."

Sounded easy enough. "Last I heard, Skaros was completely lawless." I was no pirate. My self-defense skills were limited. Okay, non-existent. "What's keeping someone from killing me before I reach the spaceship?"

"Be very careful."

That was a given.

Mom's gasping cough echoed in my mind, shoving aside my urge to tell this alien no. There was more to this mission than he was sharing.

Before I could question him further, he spun and

scurried down the hall, disappearing into the flickering blackness.

To reach the Skaros Space Station, I opted to ride in stasis rather than subject myself to the tubes necessary to manage excretion while lying awake in a capsule for even such a short time.

Thankfully, new tech meant it only took two days to travel half a light year, which was confusing if you dwelled on it too long, so I didn't.

I woke to a black tube surrounding my pod. A grinding, churning sound told me I was being pulled onto Skaros. Good. Things were going just as expected. It shouldn't take long to board the ship, steal the artifact, and activate my com. I'd be on my way back to Earth by the end of the day with enough money to cure Mom.

The capsule came to a jarring halt, and lights bloomed around me. Bangs rang out when the station's outer hatch doors slammed shut. Mechanical arms opened the top of my pod, and I bailed over the side.

A quick check showed the knife I'd strapped to my waist was still with me. It wasn't much, but I was no crack shot with a laser pistol. I might live in a city where laser shootouts were a regular occurrence, but I once read knives and fists were the easiest weapons in a pinch. Since I wasn't much of a fighter, I usually turned and bolted.

I wasn't stupid. Skaros was a pirate port floating in

space. Anything could happen to a slip of an Earthling woman like me—hence me dressing like a boy and strapping on a blade. With shorn hair, bound breasts, and loose, nondescript clothing, I'd pass casual scrutiny and have a way to defend myself if I slipped up and was discovered.

With my heart thumping heavily, I zipped around droids dismantling the capsule. Each part would find a new home, including me on Snuggles. I still couldn't believe a pirate named their spaceship something like that.

In no time, I was weaving through the main section of the space station. Sweaty aliens crowded around me, their skin, scales, and fur overheating from the solar rays shooting through the clear top of the structure. Three suns shone down on the port, and the management had taken advantage of them to generate passive heat. Panels on the outer walls gathered rays to generate power.

I could only identify a quarter of the species around me. Everyone wore weapons and a flinty challenge filled their eyes. Most clutched bags holding their worldly possessions, snarling at anyone who came near enough to try to steal.

In the city where I grew up, a pickpocket caught in action might be fined. Here, they'd lose their hand or head, the alien doling out the punishment without bothering to call the authorities—assuming there were any on board. It was easier to deal with it themselves.

"Snuggles," I whispered into my com. "Where is

Snuggles docked?" My com should be able to tap into Skaros's mainframe computer and locate the ship.

Bingo. Directions flashed on the screen along with a convenient map with a blinking dot indicating the spaceship.

I scooted around those selling wares and a few tussles with fur and bits of claws flying, leaping over the carcass of a downed alien at least twice. Drugged or dead, I couldn't determine, and I wasn't about to tap on shoulders to find out.

My com notified me Snuggles was getting ready to depart the port.

Bolting toward where it was docked, adrenaline gave me wings. I flew past aliens trying to grab my attention and scurried away from those who slashed out when I inadvertently knocked them into storefronts.

A minue later, I skidded into the hangar and ducked behind a pile of storage containers, watching as a droid crew finished loading the ship. Lo and behold—Snuggles was written in swirly script on the side of the ship.

How was I going to get on board? Back on the Plushier Space Station, this job sounded relatively easy. Now, I wasn't sure. But I couldn't back out now. There'd be no return ticket until I had the statue in hand.

I watched the droids zipping up and down the ramp loaded with boxes. Eventually, the piles of supplies waiting nearby had been brought on board. I'd yet to see any people working on the ship. Had I lucked out with a ship run solely by machines? Most droids were programmed to complete tasks. They'd ignore anything and anyone else as long as they didn't interfere with the mission. I could stroll on board among them without a care.

When the station droids finished, they filed out of the loading dock.

I took a chance, dashing across the open area between the shipping containers and the ship, and raced up the ramp. At the top, I peered around and, seeing no one, I spied a door marked Janitor's Closet halfway down the hall on my left.

Time to hide until the ship left port. I'd wait until night, creep out and find the main stateroom, steal the artifact, and activate my com. Easy.

The door whisked open at my touch, and I tumbled inside, tangling among various cleaning tools and products and nearly smacking my head on the inner wall.

After clearing a small place on the floor with the side of my foot, I dropped down, scrunched my legs up to my chest, and wrapped my arms around them. I waited for the ship to leave Skaros. Until I could determine if anyone live worked on board, it paid to be cautious. No need to rush to the stateroom and get caught.

It wasn't long before the low rumble of destar generators told me the ship was unhooking from the dock. A floaty feeling made my belly surge up into my throat, but I shoved it back down with a swallow.

A weightless feeling told me the ship drifted away from Skaros. This was followed by the engines engaging. The room vibrated subtly, making the cleaning tools rattle, reminding me I rode in a pirate ship, not a smooth charter spacecraft where I couldn't even tell the vessel was moving.

I dozed, waking periodically and hearing nothing. Excitement burst inside me. Maybe there were no people on board! Sitting with my head tipped back, I listened. No voices. No one passing by the closet. The ship must be operated by droids. I'd give it a little longer, then I'd locate the captain's stateroom and break into the safe.

Sleeping, I dreamed of returning home and buying the cure for Mom. She wouldn't be sick anymore. I wouldn't lose her.

I woke sometime later in utter silence.

When I deemed I'd remained hidden long enough, I crept from the closet and continued down the hall, cautiously opening each door I passed, but not finding anything that looked like a main stateroom. This was a big ship, however, so it might not be located on this level. Only the low hum of the engines and the shallow slap of my shoes on the floor broke the silence.

I was hugging the wall, approaching an intersection, when a bang rang out ahead. Shrinking into my skin, I wrangled with my spit, too afraid to swallow in case it was overheard.

The sound wasn't repeated, telling me it could be nothing. Space debris hitting the outer hull. A droid smacking against a wall.

With my nerve endings twitching, I pulled my knife, the weight of it giving me the boost of courage I needed to continue forward.

Muffled voices echoed from a location I couldn't

define, someone telling another person they were going to the galley.

Shit. There were people—*aliens*—on the ship!

Determined to hide, I flew to the intersection and raced around the corner.

I smacked into something big and warm and full of snarls. Huge bronze hands groped for my arms.

A shriek burst from me, and I flailed, reeling backward. I stared up at a freakin' ogre.

I only caught glimpses of burnished copper skin, an eye patch, and silver hair as he swept out his booted foot, nearly taking my legs out from underneath me.

With a guttural cry, I hitched my knife forward. It sunk into flesh, and the fuming alien ogre groaned. Dralian species, if I wasn't mistaken. They'd gotten caught up in the human-Evarian war and their people were nearly wiped out. It looked like I was doing my best to eliminate another.

And man, was this Dralian male pissed. He sputtered and fumed, glaring at me while clutching my forearm.

A blue and white fluffy creature sat on his right shoulder, watching me with sapphire blue eyes. It hissed in my direction, but who could blame it?

While I guppy breathed, the muscular alien yanked aside a corner of his sleeveless leather vest, revealing rows of rippling muscles. Man, what pecs! Leave it to me to notice at a time like this.

Blood seeped around my blade still embedded in the right side of his belly. Such a shame to ruin his washboard perfection.

He wrenched out the knife and tucked it into the waistband of his low-slung pants.

His glare from his unpatched eye pinned me in place.

"Sorry?" I whimpered, wiggling to break free from his grip. "I didn't mean to poke you."

He jerked me against his taut frame. With a simple flex, he tossed me onto his left shoulder. The fluffy cat-like creature leaned around the alien's head, its whiskers twitching. It released a long series of howls until the alien stroked the creature's spine.

Pivoting, the Dralian ogre strode down the hall, leaving a trail of amber blood droplets on the plexi floor.

"You, human youngling," he snarled. "Are about to get your ass smacked."

CHAPTER TWO
MATIS

I would never harm a youngling, even one who'd stowed aboard my ship. But damn . . . How dare he steal onto my ship and attack me?

The puny puncture the boy had made in my side with his knife wasn't much worse than the bite of a fleetzer, and I had to admire the youngling's attempt at defense. Spunk like that should be rewarded—after I'd shown him that he should never randomly stab anyone with a blade. Next time, he might hurt someone.

Entering my cabin, I locked the door and tossed the boy onto the floor. While he scrambled away from me on his ass, I wrenched off my eye patch—part of my disguise—and gently lifted Snuggles off my shoulder and placed him on my bed. His fluffy tail whipped up, and he hissed at the youngling who'd backed all the way to the wall.

"How old are you?" I asked him.

"Sixteen," he snarled in a low, squeaky voice.

I was glad the days of my voice betraying me in such a way were over.

"You look too skinny to be sixteen," I said.

"Humans aren't all huge, you know," the boy said. His voice shook, but his gaze met mine. I admired the cockiness he used to hide his fear. It would serve him well as he aged.

I'd met my share of humans while growing up in an orphanage that catered to all species. I supposed this youngling could be sixteen if he hadn't eaten right.

Like when I found Snuggles backed into a corner of an alley on Skaros, wounded and hissing with pain, a pang shot through my chest at the thought that this youngling could be starving. My sister might call me a sucker for a creature in need, and she'd be right. I was a magnet to those who needed my help.

The boy peered around the cabin.

The interior was sleek and modern, just the way I like it. The ship itself might appear to be held together with bandi cables and spit, but inside my quarters, where I retreated at the end of the day, I'd created a place where I could relax and be myself.

One wall was lined with shelves, though they contained impersonal things I'd collected at various ports. This was a job, and a dangerous one at that. I never knew when I might need to suddenly abandon ship. Why collect things I'd hate leaving behind?

Leaning back against the plexi door, I tried not to laugh as I caught the youngling gazing around frantically.

"You won't find a weapon," I said.

He scowled my way before he took in the room many would consider much too generous even for a pirate starship's captain.

My bed was larger than most, but I was a big guy and I liked stretching out. In this, I'd indulged my love of fine things, covering the bed with good sheets and luxurious blankets.

A desk and chair sat near the right wall, and I'd placed them there so I could look out the round porthole on the outer wall. When I wasn't worried about someone trying to wring my neck, it was nice to relax and take in the view. When I was young, I dreamed about traveling through the stars. Now, as an interstellar agent, I'd been given that chance.

Other than the desk and the bed, a wardrobe took up the left wall, mounted in place to keep it from toppling if travel got rough.

A few pictures hung on the walls, and a second porthole to the left of my bed hid a small safe where I kept things no one sneaking on board should discover. Fortunately, only I and the other crewmember, Firoh, knew the code. If something permanent happened to us, our coms would send a signal, and the safe would destroy the contents.

Crossing the small but cozy space, I hauled my chair away from my desk and sat. Snuggles blinked my way before glaring at the youngling. He'd warm up if the youth didn't attack again.

Tools and parts lay littered across the desk's surface. I

opened the top drawer and swept it all inside, then leaned back in my chair and propped my heels on the top of my desk. Watching the youngling, I pondered what to do with him. If someone hadn't helped me when I was young, who knew where I'd be now?

I tugged the small med kit off the shelf to my left and opened it on my lap. It didn't take long to close my belly wound with a sealer. I gave myself an antibiotic zap for good measure. A male could never be too careful.

"What's your name?" I asked.

"I don't give it to no one." The boy crossed his arms on his chest and hefted his slender chin. I had to hand it to him—he had guts considering I was the one in full control of the situation.

He reminded me a bit of myself when I took my first interstellar interpol assignment. I'd been full of cocky confidence and snark, but I got the first kicked out of me during a fight with three Vessars. There was nothing like wrangling with a lizard mafia pack to set a guy on the right track. As for the snark, I'd held onto that.

"I like to know the name of the person I'm killing before I do it," I said blandly. To add to my murderous pirate impression, I pulled his knife and started using it to clean my claws. The ones on my fingers retracted, which came in handy when I needed to pick up small objects.

The boy blanched, and I held in a feral grin.

"You'll have to beat my name out of me," he said defiantly. Rising to his feet, he clung to the wall, watching me like a coohine being stalked by a minzir.

"It appears we've come to an impasse," I said. "Here I was, about to offer you a position on my illustrious ship—"

He snorted. "Zistarn trap from what I've seen."

"At least I own a ship," I said blandly.

He snorted.

I ignored his insult. The ship might look like it was falling apart, but it had been carefully crafted to give that impression. Beneath a cloaking device, the ship gleamed, a vessel operated by the most advanced tech in the inter-galaxies. I used it during assignments, but I'd paid for its construction myself, preferring to know every square hilacart of whatever vessel I used to travel through space.

"I meant I was considering offering you a job so you can redeem yourself," I said, wondering why I couldn't seem to ignore the urge to help him. "But if you'd rather I killed you," I dropped my boots to the floor with a heavy thud and rose to tower over the boy, "I'm more than happy to do so."

"No," the youngling cried, grabbing a well-cut stone the size of his fist from the shelf. He brandished it as if he'd clunk me on the head with it. Like I'd give him the chance? One wound was enough for this dia. "Don't. I . . . My mom—" With a shake of his head, he cut off whatever he was going to say, his narrow shoulders deflating. "Please don't kill me."

"Name?" I barked.

"Tatum."

Rather girlish, but who was I to comment about

what a parent might choose for a child? "See? That wasn't hard now, was it? I'm Matis."

"Matis what?"

"Matis who will wring your neck if you don't behave." My low chuckle rang out. My sister would see right away I was teasing.

Tatum scowled.

Rounding my desk, I approached him.

His gaze went frantic, but I slipped the blade into the back waistband of my pants. Being armed in ways most wouldn't notice—though I more often relied on my brawn and fists—I didn't need such a tiny thing for defense.

I held out my hand. "Well, then, Tatum, welcome on board the Starship Snuggles."

He stared at my hand, not taking it. "That's a stupid name for a ship."

Snuggles, who'd curled up on my bed, hissed and spat in the youngling's direction. Tatum darted to the side to avoid the tiny goblet of spit. At this rate, my cabin would be coated in slime.

"Enough," I told Snuggles, though gently.

Peeling his lips back to show off his impressive, though tiny fangs, Snuggles huffed. He curled around a few times and settled on my pillow, something he knew I didn't like because he shed all the time. I'd boot him off later.

"What kind of job would you want me to do?" the youngling asked, watching Snuggles. "Because I won't be warming your bed."

I sneered. "That's the last thing I'd ever ask *you* to do."

Tatum grunted and linked his arms across his chest. The flesh above the top of his shirt bunched up oddly. When he caught me staring, he yanked the fabric all the way to his chin.

"I need a cabin boy," I said. Truly, I didn't. I should turn my ship around and leave this bit of flotsam on Skaros, but I couldn't. Maybe it was the shadows in the youngling's eyes that brought back memories of finding my family dead in our home. He appeared as lost as I'd felt back then.

Or maybe I was getting even softer as I aged—something my sister would point out with a rueful shake of her head.

"What tasks would you expect me to do?" he asked.

"Keep the place clean."

"I don't wash undergarments for no one," he barked.

"I don't wear them."

"Gross," Tatum said with a twist of his lips that were too . . . feminine for his face. Come to think of it, his features were too female overall, from his heart-shaped face to his delicate chin. Poor kid. He might grow into a larger build, but many would call him pretty.

"It's comfortable going without," I said, then checked myself. I didn't have to explain anything to this zistarn. "Collect my meals in the galley and take away the dishes after."

What else could I assign him? I purposefully hadn't brought a cabin boy on board. My mission could cost me my life. I'd never endanger a child, not even an ornery one like Tatum.

"Keep things tidy," I added, frowning. "And watch my back."

"You'd trust me not to knife you again?" he asked with wide eyes.

"Not particularly, but I imagine you can be trained to behave."

His mouth twisted at my dig.

I took in his long lashes framing eyes the color of tessamist leaves. This youth was far too delicate to survive in outer space. All the more reason to protect him.

Before my mission was through, I'd either drop him off at the orphanage where the Aunties could finish raising him or find a colony on a peaceful planet and give him enough credits to start a new—and placid—life.

Tatum scanned the room, and if I wasn't innately suspicious, I would've dismissed his glance as one of mere curiosity. Why did he appear to be searching for something?

I shrugged it off when he returned his gaze to me and gave me a curt nod.

"I guess I can do those tasks," he said. "It looks like you've hired yourself a cabin boy."

CHAPTER THREE

TATUM

There were worse jobs than serving as a cabin boy to a cocky space pirate. Best of all, I could search his cabin while he was away and find the statue. This must be the main stateroom.

A few taps of my com, and this chapter of my life would be over.

"Your first duty is to clean Snuggles's box," Matis said.

"Box of what?" I asked, bumping off the wall. So far, I hadn't seen an obvious safe, but he was a pirate. Everyone knew decent pirates hid things like that—though I doubted there were any "decent" pirates in all the galaxies. His rep as a scoundrel alone must precede him. I'd have to watch my back and sleep with one eye open.

"His refuse box," he said, dropping back into his chair. He kicked his boots up onto his desk and watched me with hooded eyes.

Tingles flashed across my skin, which should feel unpleasant. Why didn't they? I didn't like that I was hyperaware of him.

It was because I feared him, that was it. Not because . . .

A growl ripped from me, echoed by a hiss and a long howl from Snuggles—the alien fluffball fiend.

"Problems already?" Matis asked with a sneer I should find surly and pirate-like. Instead, it came out . . . . No, not sexy. I wasn't attracted to this guy. "If you're not willing to do simple tasks like caring for Snuggles—"

"No," burst from me. "I can deal with your . . . What is that thing anyway?" I glared at Snuggles who snarled and slashed out with his big paw full of claws. In addition to watching my back with Matis, I'd need to take care with Snuggles or I'd lose a finger.

"He's a charcoo," Matis said, watching me like he expected me to flee. "And he's precious to me. Do not harm or threaten him, or you will face my wrath."

"Consider me placid when it comes to Snuggles," I said with a roll of my eyes. I tightened my jaw. "Where's his box?"

"Over there." He waved toward a closet door I'd missed. Truly, I needed to pay more attention. The safe could be inside the small space.

"Anything else you'd like me to do?" I asked, trotting in that direction, which thankfully put me beyond claws-reach of Snuggles.

"After taking care of that, go to the galley and get me

something to eat. Anything will do. You'll find Firoh working there. He's also my pilot."

"A cook as well as a pilot? Talk about multi-tasking."

He grunted.

Closet, then galley. Ironically, space pirates used many of the same terms as those used by ancient Earthlings, probably because some of the earliest Earth interstellar travelers had been pirates themselves. While there also must've been aliens pirating among the stars back then, the lingo spread to them as well.

After sending him a nod, I ducked into the small closet and partly closed the door. I was grateful to be out from under his heavy gaze. It made sense he'd watch me. I'd stolen on board and for all he knew, I came here for a nefarious purpose—which I had. He might act casual with me, but I expected he'd keep an eye on me for a while before handing over even a smidgen of trust. That was okay. I wasn't going to remain here long enough for anything like that to develop.

I scooped charcoo poop into a small bucket, grimacing but not saying anything. Despite my wish to leave this ship before the dia was through, I'd likely be here for a short time. Might as well earn my keep. I didn't steal from anyone, and I wouldn't start with Matis.

Well, other than stealing the statue, that is.

The thought of being branded a thief by him scorched across the inside of my belly, but what else could I do? I wasn't going to let my mom die.

While I continued to scrape in the box, I peered around, looking for the safe.

Shelves along the back wall, barely wider than Matis's shoulders, held plexi boxes with various tools. One held laser pistols and charges, but as tempting as it would be to grab one and hide it beneath my clothing, I resisted. I sensed he was watching even if he couldn't see me inside this tiny space. He'd wait for me to do something wrong, then rain punishment down on me.

Not a beating, per se, or even the outright murder he'd taunted me with earlier. I sensed his snarly demeanor hid a squishy inside. I doubted he'd starve or lock me up in whatever served as the ship's brig. But he'd find some way to make sure I paid. He wouldn't be a good pirate if he let anything slip.

"Where should I dump this?" I asked, emerging from the closet with the bucket.

"There's a chute in the hall on the right. The code's 311. Dump it in there and the ship will process it."

Interesting. Few ships had processing units on board. Did they have one for water? Probably. From the vessel's appearance, I hadn't expected anything like that.

"Where's . . . uh, a refuse unit I can use?" I asked, pinching my legs together. Our bodies made their needs known at the most inconvenient times.

His brow scrunched before smoothing. "If you need to use the facilities, they're through that door." He waved to another panel I'd missed.

I left the bucket near the outer door and crept across his room, keeping a solid distance between me and Snuggle pain-in-the-butt, who watched me raptly. I eased around what looked like a large tank, though I had no idea why he had it parked in the corner of his room, and entered the evacuation chamber. It was almost as tiny as the closet and contained a toilet and a small hand sanitizer unit hanging from the wall. No cleansing unit but maybe the pirate captain didn't bathe. He didn't smell, but I hadn't cozied up to him to make a solid determination.

It might get stinky in his cabin. Without a cleansing unit, I couldn't bathe either.

Finishing in the tiny room, I grabbed the bucket and dumped the contents into the chute in the hall. I placed the bucket inside the closet again and used the hand cleaner.

"What level is the galley on?" I asked.

Matis was pouring over holoimages projected by his wrist com. They looked like some kind of engine or machine, but mechanical stuff wasn't my strong suit. "First floor. There are three levels on the ship. As you may have noted, we're currently on the second. Crew quarters are also on this level, though there's only Firoh and me on board. I run the ship with a light team of two, plus droids to load or offload supplies. The upper level is small and is taken up by the bridge."

"Why don't you fly your own ship instead of using a pilot?" I asked, standing in the open doorway to the hall.

"Because Firoh's a better pilot than me."

"And he cooks."

"I don't like droid cooking. It lacks flavor. Firoh makes a mean tristeen. Maybe you'll get to try it."

I doubted I'd be here long enough to sample soup.

"He's also great at covering my back if I'm stuck in a twitchy situation."

I snorted. He was a pirate; he'd need all the help he could get.

"And now we have you on board," he added. "That's it other than Snuggles."

If I was a true teenage boy and was told I was now one-third of the crew, I'd feel grateful. He'd taken a kid under his wing, more or less, and given him a job when I suspected he wouldn't otherwise hire someone.

Too bad I didn't need a job.

"Thank you," I said just to get it out there.

He looked up, his fingers hovering over one of the holoimages he'd been twisting to view at all angles. "For what?"

"Giving me a chance. For not jettisoning me into outer space."

His low chuckle rang out, coasting across my bones like the smoothest cloutine. "Behave, and I won't regret my decision."

I nodded and left, taking the stairs down one level and allowing my nose to guide me to the galley. I stood in the entrance, watching Firoh sauté something on a grill. It smelled amazing. A real grill in space. Who would've thought? But Matis had said he didn't enjoy droid cooking.

I paused in the opening of the galley.

Firoh was a Chullod alien, a species who looked much like humans except they had purple skin and tails. His long silver hair was pulled back at his nape, and his tail swished back and forth to the tune he hummed. Built like Matis, meaning massive, he wore a white apron over generic pants and a t-shirt. A tattoo of a minzer took up part of his right upper arm, with the tail coiling around to the front.

He had a heavy limp on his right side. New or old injury? I sensed it wouldn't be a good thing to ask.

"Who are you?" Firoh asked, not looking my way. He flipped something in a big frying pan, and it sizzled.

"I'm Tatum. The new cabin boy."

"I'm Firoh. I didn't realize the captain planned on hiring a cabin boy."

I bit my lip, nodding. "He wants me to bring him a meal." My belly gnashed its teeth, storming around, but I wasn't going to ask for food. They'd offer, eventually. I hoped.

"Grab a tray from that cupboard." Firoh pointed with his spatula. "And two plates while you're there." He seasoned whatever yummy thing he was cooking. "Be quick about it. I need to get back to the bridge."

Gulp. "Why would you leave the bridge?"

"To cook." He turned an eyebrow-lifted look my way. "A droid can manage while I'm away. I'm the pilot of the ship, not just the cook."

"Matis mentioned that."

Firoh grunted.

I placed the tray on the counter to the right of the grill and watched as he continued to cook chunks of real meat and vegetables in the pan.

"Why doesn't Matis use a food synthesizer?" I asked.

"Everyone else does." I'd only eaten food prepared like this maybe twice in my life.

Firoh threw me a wry look. "If we had a synthesizer, that would put me out of a job, now wouldn't it?"

I leaned against the counter. "Since you're also flying the ship, I doubt it."

"Matis could fly the ship and cook and herd you, youngling, all at the same time if he wanted. By the way, Matis and I go way back, so don't think I'll tell you anything he wouldn't want to share."

"I wouldn't dream of asking."

He cocked his head my way, the silver hair he'd tied back at his nape swishing on his back. "Or maybe you would. At this point, it doesn't matter." He chuckled, a low, deep sound that a lot of females—and males—must find appealing. "As for synthesizers, we prefer real food when we can get it, so we stocked up at the space station. I love to cook. Seems like a perfect match, doesn't it, cabin boy named Tatum? Unless you can fly the ship in addition to fetching meals."

"I can't fly." I could barely fly a paper airplane. As for cooking, Mom had done her best to teach me, but the few times we could afford "real" food, I stuck to simple recipes. We used a synthesizer the majority of the time since it was cheaper.

"Maybe you should learn, cabin boy Tatum."

I wasn't sure if he was focusing on my name or me being a cabin boy, but I wasn't going to remain here long to find out. This alien was too perceptive. In the future, I'd sneak into the kitchen and grab food for the captain rather than risk Firoh discovering I was anything but a boy. Assuming I remained on board long.

"I can't cook either," I added.

"Then I hope you can clean." Firoh dished up a generous serving onto the plate and handed it to me. Standing near me, he stared, shifting off his right hip. Definitely something wrong there. "Sit. Eat fast. Don't break the plate."

With a nod, I looked down, gaping at the quantity of food he'd given me.

He must've caught my surprise. "If you're not hungry—"

"No!" I sat, digging in fast while speaking around it. "Starved."

Firoh nodded, watching me eat for a moment before turning back to the grill.

When I'd finished, he loaded a plate for Matis and added eating implements.

"I *can* clean," I said, bringing up his earlier comment.

"Good. Then you and the captain should get along splendidly." He waved his spatula. "Ale's in the dispenser on that wall. Fill one tankard, only for him. You're too young to drink anything like that."

Actually, at twenty-eight, I was more than old enough to drink ale.

"When you start sprouting hair on your face, we'll talk." He chuckled. "Then we'll take you to a decent port and get you drunk. Find you a female, if you like that, or a male if you prefer different fare."

I found it wiser not to say anything about sex. "I don't need to get drunk."

Firoh's eyebrow lifted as one unit. "Everyone needs to get drunk every now and then."

I filled a tankard of ale and placed it on the tray.

"You'll find hot and cold water dispensers. in the hall outside the captain's quarters," he said. "Take a cup with you, and you can get yourself something to drink whenever you want."

"Thanks."

The tray in hand, I returned to the captain's stateroom.

Firoh seemed like a decent guy. Even a bit attractive if I was into dark purple skin, silver hair, and a gruff, though I suspected kind, demeanor. And he liked Matis. If Matis was loyal to his crew, I might have a good chance of—

Hold on, there. I wasn't remaining on board for long. I'd locate the statue and steal it, then activate my wrist com for an evacuation. I wasn't looking to work my way up in the ranks on a ship named Snuggles.

I placed the tray on Matis's desk, then puttered around the room while he ate.

He stood after eating and waved to the big basin in the corner of his stateroom. "Fill that with hot water from the tap in the hall." He tossed aside his vest, exposing bulging muscles and long scars I wanted to ask about. Trace my fingers along. Lick.

No, not lick. I wouldn't put my tongue near any part of his body.

He undid the top button of his pants. "Hurry up there, youngling. I'm going to take a bath, and you're scrubbing my back."

CHAPTER FOUR
MATIS

I loved watching the youngling squirm, grumble, and huff. Me bathing bothered him, did it? Perhaps it was the thought of me being naked.

To think someone so innocent had survived this long in outer space.

He lugged one bucket after another into my room, filling the tub.

When I accepted this assignment from Interstellar Interpol, I had only a few conditions. I wanted to use my own ship. They had no problem with that. The ship looked like a clunker, but it had solid bones beneath the façade. I worked better when I had my own things around me, including a tub to bathe in each night, with real water. None of that cleansing unit shit for me. I'd never felt clean after being sprayed and blown dry. Nope, that only came from a good long soak in hot water. It was one of the few luxuries I didn't deny myself.

My only other condition was that I wanted to pick

my own crew. They offered one agent, Firoh, who I approved. One was skimpy of them, but with budget cuts, we were all used to getting by with less.

I'd worked with Firoh before, and he was a solid agent. The fact that he sidelined as a cook and pilot when he wasn't breaking skulls for the Agency added to his favor. He guided our course to various ports of call where I could further the investigation, plus worked with me on the assignment.

He'd been injured during a mission three yaros ago, but he didn't let the extensive wounds he'd received slow him down. If anything, he worked harder than most of us to show he could still deliver. There'd been some talk about discharging him from the agency, but he'd appealed and someone must've spoken up for him, because they dropped all talk of letting him go.

Yaros ago, Firoh worked for his government as a spaceship commander before he was tapped by Interstellar Interpol for assignments. Pilots didn't need to be able to run fast to fly.

He'd be leaving my ship soon because he needed to take over the care of his twin sons. He'd contracted with an Earth female to help her have a child, and she'd produced two. The contract specified he'd have no role in their lives, but things happen. She died, and no surviving relatives stepped forward to claim them, he'd been approached to take over their care.

The agency wasn't a place for younglings, so he'd be leaving the service.

When the tub was so full with water it nearly sloshed

across the lip, I undid the rest of the fastenings on my pants. The fabric parted.

Tatum's too-pretty eyes widened as his gaze honed in on the hint of my cock. He gasped and spun to present me his back.

"I'm probably bigger than you, youngling, but I don't possess anything you haven't seen before." I shed my pants, tossing them on top of my shirt. "Touched, probably, too."

"I don't touch myself," Tatum said in a strangled voice.

"Well, maybe you should. It might loosen you up a bit." I strolled over to the tub. "Take my clothing to the sanitizer in the hall. It's mounted in the wall to the left of the water spigots." Climbing into the water, I sunk down onto the inner seat and groaned.

Tatum turned, staring at me with his mouth ajar. "You . . ." He scrambled to grab my clothing and bolted from the room.

"Come back quick, youngling, so you can wash my back," I called after him, chuckling in a low voice.

Dunking down, I wet my hair and used the suds bar to clean it. I hummed as I scrubbed my pits and chest, splashing the water when I went for my groin. My cock remained flaccid, but at thirty-three, I'd long since established control of it. Now I only got a hard-on when I needed an outlet for stress—something I didn't avail myself of often enough.

Maybe when I next put into port . . .

Nah. As nice as it was to sink myself into someone's

welcome heat, I'd become jaded in my old age. Seeing my sister happy with my best friend, Shaede, made me long for a touch that was given because someone cared, not because they were paid to do so.

It might be nice to love someone, too, though I hadn't believed in something like that until my sister and Shaede. Their adoration for each other gave me a new perspective.

There was nothing wrong with holding myself back until I found something like that.

Snuggles hopped off the bed, shooting a hiss at the closed door. He leapt up onto the edge of the tub and dipped a toe into the water.

"You won't like it, beastie," I said with affection coloring my voice. I stroked his head and scratched beneath his chin, and his rumbling purr soon provided harmony with my humming.

Tatum scurried back into the room, looking anywhere but at me.

Maybe he preferred males, and I'd unsettled him.

"I won't take advantage of you," I said.

"I'd knife you if you did."

Speaking of which. A glance down showed the wound had sealed over; the benefit of having access to the best medical tech in the galaxies.

"I took your knife away from you," I pointed out. "There'll be no more poking."

He rolled his eyes and took in his blade lying on my desk.

"I could reach it before you," I said in warning.

"I'm not even going to try." He opened the wardrobe and put my clean clothing away.

"Back," I said.

Turning, he lounged against the wall. "Excuse me?"

I frowned at his too-cute features. I'd have to watch out for him when we made port, or someone would take advantage of his puny form and weak fighting skills.

A growl ripped through me at the thought, and Tatum must've thought that was my reply to his question.

"What? I can't ask for clarification?" he said.

"Wash my back." I pointed to the cloth draping along the edge of the tub.

With a heavy sigh, he crossed the room, giving Snuggles a wide berth. "Will he rip my arm off if I touch you?"

"Not as long as you're not holding a knife."

"I didn't see him providing much defense in the hall."

"You startled him and me. Just watch him in action sometime."

Tatum rolled his eyes. He grabbed the cloth and wet it; his eyes trained above my head. "Sit forward."

I obliged and groaned while he rubbed the cloth across my back. The swirls he made were strangely sensual. My cock stirred.

"That's enough," I half-yelled, chastising myself for being mildly aroused by my cabin boy's touch. "Find something else to do. Grab my towel."

"You can't even dry yourself?" Tatum asked, and if I'd heard much snark in his voice, I would've called him on it.

"I thought your dainty sensibilities might appreciate holding it up rather than viewing this." I stood, shedding water down my form, and stepped onto the mat lying beside the tub. Thankfully, my cock was behaving and had dropped between my thighs. It might be thinking of rising, but it hadn't taken the bait yet.

Tatum raced to the towel on a chair and tossed it to me, keeping his back facing my way.

Shaking my head, I bent over and pulled the plug, allowing the water to drain. It would be filtered, purified, and ready to use long before my next bath.

I could only hope he'd get used to seeing me nude. How else were we going to get along? I bathed. Changed my clothing. He didn't need to blush and avoid looking. This was a normal thing between a cabin boy and his captain.

But I wanted him to remain in my cabin. I only trusted him so far. The thought of letting him roam about the ship at night made me jittery.

"Take the tray back to the galley, and then we'll go to bed," I said. "You'll find powder in the closet to do your teeth." I'd do mine while he was gone.

I rubbed myself dry while he scooted from the room. Draping the towel on a hook to dry, I grabbed my powder and did my teeth, taking care to ensure my fangs were clean too. Another silly indulgence, but I liked a decent smile.

Tatum returned, keeping his eyes trained on the floor.

I opted to ignore his discomfort. He'd get used to

seeing me naked eventually, and my cock would soon realize I was not attracted to my cabin boy.

"Where will I sleep tonight?" Tatum asked.

"Here. With me."

CHAPTER FIVE
TATUM

It was bad enough he was letting his cock dangle in full view. I was struggling to get that horrifying image out of my mind; a difficult task with it on full display.

"Have you no modesty?" I growled. It was huge. Ribbed. And it made my belly clamp tight.

Okay, if I was being honest with myself, it made my ovaries quiver.

No way! I wasn't attracted to his cock. Jeez. It was a tool guys used. They'd pump it in and out a few times, groan, and shoot you full of jizz that leaked down your legs for hours. Who needed something like that?

"What's modesty?" he asked with a smirk. "This is my stateroom. I can strut around with nothing on all day long if I want."

"What if someone walked in?" I sputtered.

"Who?"

I shrugged. "Firoh?"

"He'd knock first. I could cover up. But it wouldn't be the first time he'd see me naked."

"Information I do not need to hear!"

His laugh snorted out. "We're males. Seeing shit like this happens."

"I don't care about your . . . junk." Jeez.

"And I don't care about yours."

"None of that matters. I'm not warming your bed," I barked, my wide eyes shooting to the too-soft appearing bedding.

"Like I'd let a mangy zistarn like you beneath my covers."

"I'm no zistarn." I stalked back and forth, Snuggle pain-in-the-butt swiping out to rip my arm apart each time I passed. Finally, I stopped and glared at Matis while leaning against the wall beside his desk.

"You're staring at my cock," he said. "I don't care who you love, but you need to know right now I only do females."

"I'm not interested in males." A lie. "And even if I was, I sure wouldn't be excited about you."

The grin he shot me was full of cocky confidence. "Believe me. Females rarely turn down what I have to offer."

"I don't need to hear about you catting your way across the galaxies."

"Just putting you on notice. Keep that in mind when we put into our next port. You'll need to find something safe to occupy yourself with when I head into town."

"Maybe I'll want to go into town myself."

His mood sobered. "Ports are dangerous places."

"I can defend myself, as you saw."

"You mean that little poke with your knife?" Lifting it from the table, he tossed it my way.

Before I could control my response, I squeaked and darted to the side, coming close enough to Snuggles, who snagged my sleeve.

"You were supposed to catch it. What kind of pirate cabin boy do you hope to be if you can't do something simple like that?"

"Maybe this is a temporary job for me."

"I decide the length."

"What, are you going to make me work for you until I'm a thousand yaros old?" I asked, disengaging Snuggles's claws from my sleeve before he sunk them into my flesh. He hissed and hopped off the tub, stalking to Matis's bed, where he curled up into a big ball on the pillow. With his nose tucked into his fluffy tail, he blinked my way.

"I thought you could remain on board at least three lunar cycles, but we can talk about it." He scraped his claws through his still damp hair that needed to be combed, before securing it at his nape with a strip of material. He crossed to the wardrobe and pulled out soft lounge pants to tug over his legs, thankfully covering his delectable ass and other intriguing parts. With a sigh, he sat in a comfy-looking chair parked in the corner.

He watched me like a jarvan, a hawk-like creature with rich brown feathers that matched Matis's eyes.

While he said nothing, I felt like we'd come to an impasse where only one of us would win.

Snuggles jumped off the bed and sauntered over to Matis, leaping up onto his lap. He purred and his tail puffed upward while Matis scratched his neck.

Matis's broad shoulders filled the back of the seat, and his abs rippled down to the low-slung pants. You could carve stone with his sharp jawline.

His toes were cute, even with the short claws, and it just wasn't fair. Why did he have to be so attractive? His snarly demeanor should put me off, but instead, it seemed to lure me in.

Matis confused me. He came across as a ruthless space pirate, yet I could already tell his cocky demeanor hid a squishy interior. He was kind to Snuggles and what he saw as an orphaned youngling.

"I can give you a lunar cycle," I finally said. I wouldn't be here long enough for this to matter.

"Good." He started stroking Snuggles's spine. "There are blankets in the closet. Make a bed with them in the corner."

"There must be another cabin I can use instead."

"I plan to keep an eye on you."

"Fair enough. I *did* stab you."

"I wasn't expecting to find anyone else on board." He sounded defensive, but I would be too. I'd gotten the drop on him, and I doubted he liked it. "Why did you board my ship?"

Think fast. "I needed to leave the last port."

His fingers stilled momentarily on Snuggles before he

started patting the beast again. "You didn't steal anything back there, did you?"

"Nothing like that. Your ship was convenient. It helped that you only had droids loading the cargo hold. They left, and I assumed droids also ran the ship. I was able to sneak on board easily."

"Good point. I'll post guards at the next port."

Hopefully, I'd be on my way back to Earth before he put into the next port.

"Sometime during the next few dias, I'll start training you how to defend yourself," he said.

"Alright." I'd never turn down the chance to learn self-defense skills. "Are you sure you're up to it? I mean, I'm tiny compared to you. Puny, as you so kindly pointed out. Yet I stabbed you." I was only teasing, and man was it so much fun.

His laugh burst out, a happy sound that startled me. Not because it was rich and deep and boisterous.

Because it made something unexpected bubble up inside me.

I wanted to laugh with him.

No, I wanted to shove Snuggles off his lap and take the pet's place. I wanted Matis to stroke me instead of his charcoo.

CHAPTER SIX
MATIS

I slept with one eye half-open and woke up cranky. I wasn't truly worried Tatum would attack me during the night, but I wouldn't have survived this long as an interstellar agent if I let down my guard for anyone.

Lying on my cozy bed, I contemplated how best to fit my new employee into my job within a job. The galaxies thought I was the mighty pirate captain Matis Krestrat, but beneath my swashbuckling surface, I hid Matis Es'oit, a highly trained interstellar agent on an assignment. My goal was to track down the ringleaders of a smuggling operation and find out what their operation was covering. There was more to their operation than raiding abandoned planets for artifacts to sell on the black market.

I hid one of their finds inside my safe, a clue I'd picked up six lunar cycles ago from a contact who told me to lock it up and make sure no one discovered I had it. I brought it out periodically to study it, hoping it would point me in the right direction, but it remained silent.

So far, I hadn't figured out what their operation was covering, but I suspected the Ergeepelons were involved. Or a branch in the Vessar lizard mafia's tree. My sister and my friend had recently uncovered another branch in the Vessar tree, exposing an explosive mining operation on a prison planet. I'd hoped those they eliminated and had arrested would add another piece to my enormous puzzle, but so far, it hadn't. The Vessars running the explosive operation hadn't revealed anything about my assignment, even under questioning.

When I reached the next port, however, I would meet up with an undercover Vessar agent who might have some information that would point me in the right direction. We'd dock tomorrow.

Hence me wondering what I'd do with Tatum while I met up with my contact and then spent some time storming around the port to lend credence to my pirate persona.

I could lock him inside my room or the rarely used brig on the lower level, but then I'd *really* need to watch my back when I returned. He was a tiny spitfire already. No need to rile him up further.

Rolling onto my side, a grin spread across my lips, making my cheeks ache. When had I last fully smiled? Hard to say. Maybe when I saw my sister and my best friend so happy together.

Snuggles was living up to his name. Tatum lay on his blanket nest, facing away from me, and Snuggles had flopped beside Tatum, cozying up to the youngling's back, stealing heat. When Snuggles caught me looking, he blinked slowly before pushing his snout further beneath his fluffy tail.

What would the boy think when he woke and discovered my charcoo had decided the youngling was useful as a heater?

I didn't need a cabin boy. I'd only taken him in because it seemed mean to dump him at the next port. Sure, he'd poked my side, but that was already healed. The kid had only been defending himself, and I admired his spunk.

Strangely enough, warmth for the youngling had settled into my bones. It was dangerous to build relationships while on assignment. Firoh was a friend, not just a fellow agent, but we didn't share much personal information. How could we when we could be killed in action?

That was why Firoh was leaving after this job finished—or sooner if I didn't wrap things up fast. He'd shared a little about the younglings he never anticipated raising.

It took time for the government to track Firoh down and notify him that he was the boys' sole surviving relative. He was determined to raise them, which meant leaving the force that could kill him before the boys had a chance to bond with a new parent.

The younglings would soon arrive on the Plushier Space Station, and an admin would notify Firoh so he could retrieve them.

Maybe Tatum would warm up to me, and I could guide and train him to work at the agency. He could apply to Interstellar Interpol in a few yaros and eventually take on his own assignments. I could build a father/mentor relationship with him, since it didn't appear I'd find a mate and have my own young.

If someone hadn't stepped in and helped me when I was orphaned, who knows what would've happened to me?

Tatum stirred and shifted.

Snuggles hissed, but remained where he was.

I sat up in my bed, settling my pillows behind me, eager to watch the show.

Tatum yawned, and I was struck all over again by how feminine his features were. Not everyone grew into a masculine appearance, but being so tiny and slight, I wondered how the youngling would find a mate. He'd be shorter than most, though I hadn't met many Earthlings for comparison, and size wasn't everything.

I shrugged. It wasn't my concern. That was for the boy to figure out when he reached the age he'd start looking.

Tatum turned, and his eyes opened. Slow awareness took over his expression. It was good that he'd been able to escape during sleep. We all needed a reset and rest was the best way to get it.

He yelped and scrambled away from Snuggles, who hissed and darted beneath my bed.

"He, he . . ." the boy pointed at my pet.

"He kept you warm last night, didn't he?" I said, hiding my smile.

Tatum huffed. "I don't like him."

"You don't need to. Now that you're up, go get me some breakfast and cavast. Make sure Firoh adds a little pitcher of cream for the cavast on the tray. I don't like to drink it black. And while you're there, eat." I sat up, the covers falling to my waist.

Tatum gulped and flipped onto his back so he didn't have to take in my naked chest.

"You're going to have to get over your aversion for nudity, youngling," I grumbled. "I usually wear something, but I'm not going to gain modesty just to soothe your youthful sensibilities."

Tatum rose and dashed into the evacuation chamber, my low chuckle following him. He emerged not long after, his hair combed and his clothing straightened.

I frowned at his rumpled shirt and pants. "You slept in that?"

"*I* don't strut around naked like you," he huffed.

"You should try it sometime. It's relaxing." I flung back the covers and sat on the side of the bed, planting my feet on the thin rug. Last night, I'd removed my soft lounge pants before sliding beneath the covers.

He gulped and wrenched open the door and fled into the hall.

I shook my head. When the door shut, Snuggles crept out from beneath the bed. I scooped him up and planted him on my shoulder, his favorite spot. I rose and strode into the evacuation chamber, taking care of my needs, then donned some clean pants, leaving my chest bare.

At my desk, I poured through the schematics of the Weldroolar Space Station, where my ship would put into port not long after breakfast. Space station was a generous term for the place. Pile of fused-together junk might be a more apt name.

I reviewed the scant information about the smugglers I'd poured through at least ten times, not finding anything new. So many pieces that could go into the puzzle I was trying to solve.

I uploaded the scant bit of info I'd discovered to the Agency. They'd share it with anyone who might have input.

My last contact indicated I might be able to make headway with my investigation on Weldroolar, hence tracking down someone who'd worked with the Agency before and asking him to see what he could find out before I arrived. After we put into port, I'd sell the cargo I'd collected at my last destination and buy something I could sell somewhere else to give me an excuse to dock wherever my investigation took me.

I didn't randomly buy stuff; I ensured whatever I procured was something needed by others. For all intents and purposes, me and Firoh acted as much like space pirates as anyone else in the galaxies. Even the droids weren't aware of what went on behind the scenes. If any were captured and their data searched, the person spying would find nothing unusual.

This was how most jobs went. It was hard to find

contacts who were willing to risk their lives to squeal, so a job like this took endless patience. It might take me yaros to unveil the leaders of the artifact smuggler operation, let alone discover the secret they were covering.

As far as anyone knew, I was a space pirate, not an agent playing the role. Anyone who boarded my ship would only find evidence of ongoing purchase and sales of black-market items. Even a deep search wouldn't reveal anything else. This was how we held onto our heads.

Tatum knocked on the door. Really. Did he hope this would induce me to cover myself if I already hadn't?

"Enter," I said.

He bustled into the room with a tray, and my belly rumbled at the wonderful smell. Firoh played his own role within the Agency, and he'd snoop around when we reached port unless I needed him to remain on board. But he was also a world class chef, and every dish he prepared showed his magical touch.

"Put it there," I said, pointing to my desk.

While I ate, he tidied the room.

A ping on my wrist com rang out.

"Yup," I said into the device.

"Our request to dock on the Weldroolar Space Station has been accepted," Firoh said. "You can leave the ship in, eh, I'd say twenty minues."

"Great, thanks." I ended the call and frowned at Tatum, who appeared to be studying the inner walls of my cabin with more interest than he should.

"What are you doing?" I barked.

He jumped. "Nothing. It's dusty in here. I'll, um, get a cloth and start wiping down the walls."

For whatever reason, I doubted this was why he was examining everything so closely.

Despite his irksome attitude, I liked him, and not just because he reminded me of myself at that age. There was something very appealing about him. If I wasn't solid in my sexuality, I'd think I was . . .

Fuck. I wasn't attracted to the mangy youth. People loved who they wanted, but this was a youngling, and I was no creep. Never had been and never would be.

Maybe while I was in port, I'd look up one of my female friends who was always happy to tumble into bed, females who didn't want promises, just sex.

Something I hadn't experienced in too long. My job kept me busy, and it was hard to find someone I could trust long enough to let down my guard.

"Get ready to leave the ship," I told him as I ate the nullen I'd used to gather the last of the minzer egg yolk off my plate. Grabbing my eye patch, I slipped it over my head, covering my left eye.

"What's up with that?" he asked.

"Bad eye." Not really, but the patch added to my pirate appearance.

"What are we going to do at the station?" Tatum asked, frowning my way.

"*We're* not doing much. *I* have cargo to offload, new cargo to collect, and a friend I plan to sit with in a bar with for a drink or two."

He grunted. "Why not leave me here, then?" His gaze shot to the closet and then my wardrobe.

What was he looking for? He'd told me he snuck on board because he wanted to leave the space station, but what if he had some other reason to be on my ship?

I wasn't the only spy in the galaxies, that was for sure.

A niggling feeling tickled down my spine, and I never ignored this feeling.

I scrutinized his form.

I'd assumed he was the teenager he presented himself to be, but what if there was more to Tatum than he was letting on?

CHAPTER SEVEN
TATUM

I had no desire to wander around the space station, but I'd been locked up on this clunker of a ship, dealing with this ass of a "boss" for more time than I liked.

"Leave me here," I said. "I'll be in your way on the space station." How far did I dare push this? He watched me with an intensity that made my skin quake, as if he was seeking a way into my mind. If he got in, he'd rifle through the contents and discover my secrets. "It sounds like you've got business to conduct. I could . . . clean this place." I plastered a look of disgust on my face. "It needs it."

"You'll go with me," he said.

I grumbled because he'd expected it, but sighed like I was relenting. If I didn't need to search his cabin, I'd flee the second my feet hit the space station platform.

"While we're in port," he said, "I'll get you some more clothing."

I picked at my shirt. "What I'm wearing is fine."

"In a day or so, you're going to stink, and I don't abide stink in my stateroom."

Yeah, lord your bathing rituals over me, why don't you? "Then kick me out of your room."

He grumbled. "Do as I say while we're in port, or I'll leave you there."

Panic dragged across my soul with the sharp edge of a blade. I needed to get control of my mouth or he'd boot me off the ship before I located the statue.

"I'll go with you." Ditching my sullen look, I aimed for wide-eyed and pleasant. From the narrowing of his brow, I wasn't sure how successful I was. I was no actor. "I'll stick close. You can get me some clothing. Add them to my tab."

I couldn't wear this outfit much longer if I needed to remain on board. It hadn't occurred to me to bring a bag. I thought I'd find the stature and leave within minues.

"Consider clothing as something that comes with the job," he said. His face softened. Did he see me as a pity case? I squirmed, though I kept the feeling beneath my skin. I didn't need him to respect or like me, just treat me civilly. "I'll give you a few credits while we're there. Buy yourself something fun," he added.

"Fun?"

"Well, not sex. You're too young."

Heat rose in my face, and he frowned. I had to be careful or he'd see right through my disguise. Did teenage boys blush? Probably. I needed to project a very naïve personality, or he'd become suspicious.

"You don't need to give me credits," I said.

"But I will." He waved to the tray. "Get rid of this and meet me back here."

I left the room with the tray, taking it to the galley. Firoh had left, and the sanitizer hummed, washing and drying the dirty dishes. When it stopped, I pulled everything out, put them away—it was a small kitchen and easy to find my way around—and placed Matis's dishes inside the unit. After pressing a few buttons, it started humming again. I darted back into the captain's room just as his wrist com pinged.

"Docking sequence has commenced," a mechanical voice said.

Matis rose and tossed on a shirt, leaving it half unbuttoned and topping it with a thick, laser-proof vest. He unlocked a weapon's cabinet and while he armed himself to the teeth, then hid a few more weapons on his person, I pretended to dust with an old sock, moving close enough to the cabinet to look inside. No safe.

Matis would keep important things well hidden.

After he hefted Snuggles and placed the beast on his shoulder, we left, him locking the room behind with a thumb scan.

"You should program that for me so I can enter when you're not around," I said, struggling to sound cheery and helpful. That was me, cabin boy extraordinaire. I'd be his beloved pet—usurping Snuggles's place—before his ship pulled into the next port.

"Why would I want you inside my room when I'm not there?" he asked, striding down the hall.

I half-jogged to keep with his long strides while Snuggles watched with mockery gleaming in his blue eyes. "So I can get your bath ready before you arrive. Have meals waiting. Straighten everything."

"You can do that when I'm there. I don't leave the ship often."

Okay. This job was presenting a challenge. No wonder the alien was paying so much.

In a few minue, I stood in the loading dock shifting my feet and darting my eyes toward the hatch that would soon open. I'd spent all my life on Earth and had no idea what to expect on a pirate space station. I hadn't spent much time on Skaros, because I'd immediately headed for the ship.

"Stop fidgeting," Matis said.

Snuggles hissed.

It was all I could to avoid hissing back. "I'm not." But I made myself hold still.

Matis pulled the knife I'd gouged his belly with from his waistband and offered it to me. "Take this."

I blinked down at it.

"Your eyelashes are too long," he said.

I flashed a look up at him. "What?"

"Your lashes. They're too feminine. Your shape too. We need to bulk you up."

"Excuse me?" I sputtered.

"Lift weights. Do some physical activity to build even a scrap of muscle." He latched onto my upper arm and squeezed it, huffing. "Look at this. Sixteen and still puny."

Fear scraped the fine hairs off my skin. I wrenched away from him. "The, uh, men in my family are small boned."

His lips twisted. "I'll have to watch out for you. Someone will spy your pretty face and try to steal you." He barked out a laugh, but the humor didn't reach his eyes that continued to study me.

"I can't help what I look like," I gulped out. Jeez. Could I take the blade to my lashes? I couldn't change my feminine features.

"Keep the knife handy. When we get back to the ship, you can help the droids load cargo. That'll give you a start to building some muscle mass. If someone tried to take advantage of you, you wouldn't be able to put up a fight."

"You trust me with the knife?" I asked.

He grunted, and I took it, tucking it into the waist-band of my pants.

The hatch opened, and we strode down the ramp and onto one of the many docks on the space station.

A droid zipped over to hover in front of Matis. It didn't take long for him to negotiate the sale of his cargo. I marveled at how he sought a price that was much larger than the original offer and got it.

They started bickering about the new cargo he'd purchase and have loaded in the ship's hull.

I peered around the dock. If I could locate the statue when we returned to his room, I could flee the ship. Then I could activate my com for a pickup. I wouldn't have to see Matis again.

"Pay attention, youngling," Matis barked. "You might learn something."

"I'll never be a pirate."

"There are worse jobs in the galaxies."

They continued negotiating the cargo until they'd agreed on quantity and price.

"Come," Matis told me, striding away from his ship, Snuggles bobbing on his shoulder with his sharp gaze taking everything in.

I trotted after Matis.

"The cargo I just purchased will fetch a decent price in the Wondron Sector," he said. "There, I'll buy something else."

"How do you know what one place will buy?"

"Spies."

I snorted, but his face remained serious. His intent gaze swept the area as we passed huge crates full of goods and aliens puttering about. We entered a hall with a door at the end leading to the main part of the space station.

"Who's spying for you?" I asked. He seemed like a decent if irksome person. I supposed he had friends. One of them might tip him off to what one space station or planet needed.

"Whoever I can bribe."

Why was I not surprised?

"Will Firoh remain on the ship?" I asked casually as he pressed his thumb on the panel beside the door. It swept open, and we were greeted by a long hall leading in both directions. The low hum of many voices and the stomping of feet and paws echoed from our right.

Pausing, he frowned down at me. "Why does this matter?"

"I'm just making conversation."

He began walking again, casually stroking Snuggles, who leaned into his touch and purred. "Firoh has to check in on his twin sons."

"They live here?"

"They've been living on Earth with their mother, but she died. He's taking over their care once they arrive."

"No one's sending them here, are they?" I asked, my eyes widening as we passed an eight-legged alien that too closely resembled an enormous green centipede for my comfort. It ignored us other than one of its antennae bobbing out to touch Matis's arm and then mine.

Snuggles raked the centipede with his claws, and the creature shrieked.

Matis snarled as the centipede scurried away.

"Watch out for Poosines. They're known to plant," he wrenched something off his arm and held it out in his palm, "trackers." Dropping it to the tile floor, he crushed it beneath his boot. A pinch, and he'd removed the one off my arm, destroying it too.

"What kind of tracker?" I gaped at the bits of metal lying on the floor.

"Trafficking exists everywhere, but your odds of being scooped up are greater here than in other locations." He continued down the hall. "The tracker secretes a drug that disables you, and once you're unresponsive, the Poosine will use it to find you. By the time you wake, you'll be locked in a cage and on your way to an auction."

Shuddering, I nodded to Snuggles, thanking him for his defense, though he'd protected Matis, not me.

Snuggles jerked his gaze away from mine.

"As for Firoh's sons, no," Matis said, "he'll pick them up in a better place than this."

We entered a busy alley and passed people lying along the outer wall, scraps of garbage, though very little was useless in a space station, and a few mangy aliens selling drugs.

"Stay close to me," Matis barked as he strode out into a larger hall. Various species jostled around us.

"I'm fine," I said with a twist of my lips. "You don't need to watch out for—"

He latched onto my arm and dragged me against his side while ripping my knife away from a multi-limbed Bretak before the male could tuck it into his pocket. I hadn't even felt the alien take it.

With a scowl, Matis handed back my blade. "Pay attention."

My shoulders curled forward, and I blushed.

Damn, I needed to figure out how to keep my face from overheating so much. "Sorry."

The Bretak bared his fangs and his bright pink skin darkened. His ancestors could rip off a troolon's leg with one bite, which was saying something since troolons were about fifteen Earth feet tall.

Matis took one step toward the Bretak, a growl ripping up his throat. Snuggles swiped out.

The Bretak reeled backward, hitting the metal wall, and slunk into the crowd.

Turning, Matis kept going, traveling down one alley after another, each wider than the last, like we traversed spokes in a wheel, and we were headed for the big open central hub. Tiny living quarters and a few shops lined the alleys, though I didn't see many customers when I peeked through one barred plexi window.

We emerged into an enormous marketplace. A clear plexi dome arched overhead, showing off the stars and a few moons gleaming in the distance.

The market bustled with strange sights and sounds. Alien vendors hawked wares wherever I looked, their voices drowned out by the constant din of the crowds.

The stalls and shops were filled with everything I could imagine and then some, from glowing crystals and shimmering fabrics to pungent spices and small caged animals. The aroma of sweat and spices hung thickly in the air, and the sound of haggling and bargaining rang out from every direction.

In the distance, a group of reptilian creatures huddled around a small petro blaze, roasting something on a spit. The smell of cooking flesh wafted through the air.

Anything could be bought and sold here, no matter how illegal or illicit it might be. The danger and excitement of this place sparked through my veins like the finest liquor.

Creatures of all shapes and sizes surrounded us, some with multiple eyes, others with tentacles, and some with unidentifiable appendages. Vendors called out to anyone passing by, some stuffing items for sale in aliens' faces.

I turned to a tap on my shoulder, finding a short, rodent-like creature holding out a small tray of food. "Take one."

"Don't," Matis said with a shake of his head, tugging me away by my sleeve. "Don't touch anything and don't talk to anyone. Those "treats" will introduce you to a new drug, addicting you immediately. Then they can demand whatever price they want for more."

"Okay," I gulped, grateful he was with me. Despite my strong will and determination, there was no way I could protect myself here. I'd become fodder within minues.

"Where are we going?" I asked as he wove through the crowd.

His hand lifted toward a sign swinging outside an establishment recessed into the outer wall of the market. "I'm meeting a friend at the Widow's Black Hole."

An interesting name for a seedy bar if I'd ever heard one.

"Wait out here," he said, once we stood out front. He peered around, his one-eyed glare making a few aliens yelp and back away.

"Why can't I go inside with you?" I asked. Pirate business, most likely. "Are you going to do something you shouldn't?"

He scowled. "What I do inside is none of your business. Pull your knife and find a place to hide."

A glance around only revealed a dumpster.

Ugh.

CHAPTER EIGHT

MATIS

I didn't want to leave the youngling outside the bar, but I didn't trust him. I needed to meet my contact as part of my Interpol job, not something related to my cover as a pirate. The latter, I might allow him to overhear. The former? Nope.

I'd be quick. He'd barely realize I was gone.

I lifted Snuggles off my shoulder and placed him on the Tatum's shoulder. "Keep an eye on my pet."

Snuggles reeled back from Tatum's head, hissing.

Tatum hissed back.

Snuggles dug his claws into Tatum's hide.

"You two," I barked. "Behave."

Tatum scowled. Snuggles sighed.

Tatum tightened his grip on his knife and slunk into the alley and behind the dumpster, ducking down. I watched the surrounding area, and when I was sure no one was paying attention to the dumpster, I ducked through the bar's entrance.

Inside, I lurked in the shadows while assessing the room.

Stairs led up from the left side of the open bar to the second level where they rented a few rooms by the horus. A hall snaked off on the right with a small kitchen at the end, plus a multi-gender bathroom and an exit. I'd avoid the bathroom unless absolutely necessary. This was my curse for enjoying nice things; I didn't use facilities that stunk worse than a teetredon. The rest of the barroom was taken up by metal tables where a variety of clientele sat, drinking or gaming, some staring off into space.

This was one of many bars on the space station, and this one was no worse or nicer than the rest. As usual, the atmosphere could lull you with the soft music playing in the background modified with subliminal messages to "remain calm," plus lighting crafted to induce relaxation. They didn't want anyone falling asleep, but the owner did want to avoid fights. Rowdy patrons were shoved out the door, and acts of violence were mostly frowned upon, but only because they got blood on the floor.

I resisted pinching my nose, and breathed through my mouth as I was assaulted by the odor of brugeer smoke, sour sweat, and rot-gut liquor—the latter brewed on site.

Scanning the room, I sought my contact. The sooner I got the information I needed, the quicker I could get out of here.

Three orange-skinned Sevests sat at a nearby table playing juveetier with a tall Aegrin, while a variety of multi-limbed aliens leaned against or sat at the long metal bar.

A Brevule tended the bar, her blue skin gleaming in the low light. She flashed her three-inch tusks as she slid a drink over to one of the patrons.

The Aegrin bellowed and stood, having won the match. The Sevests snarled and rose as well, one leaping across the table to tackle the Aegrin, dragging them to the floor.

The bartender pulled a pistol and shot, hitting one of the Sevests in the spine. Plunging to the floor, the alien twitched. His companions hefted him beneath his arms and dragged him from the bar while the Aegrin scrambled to collect her winnings and leave.

Other tables held one or two aliens, some speaking, others staring sullenly into their drinks.

A lone Vessar sat in the right corner closest to the door, facing the room. His gaze met mine before he looked down at the book he had open on the table.

Once she'd tucked her pistol into the back of her pants and gotten back to work, I waved for the bartender to bring me a drink. No need to place a fancy order. They only served the brew they concocted here. I wouldn't drink it, but it did provide great cover.

Meandering over to the Vessar, I leaned against the wall beside him where I could keep an eye on everyone else.

"Good book?" I said.

"Have you read Duliard?" he asked.

"Only a little. A poet, right?"

"No, he writes long treatises about battle."

"I'm mistaken, then," I said, sticking with the lines I'd memorized from my latest Interpol missive. "I could swear he wrote flowery poetry."

The Vessar waved to one of the empty seats at his table. "Sit, friend, and I'll tell you about Duliard."

I dropped down into the chair, and the Vessar tucked his long, lizard snout close to his chest to make it difficult for anyone watching to read his lips. He laid his left hand with long, sharp claws onto the book, but before he could say anything, the bartender brought me my drink. I held up my wrist com for her to scan, and she took the payment electronically.

Her gaze passed over us sullenly, but I doubted she'd remember much about us once she returned to the bar. Unless we made a fuss, she'd ignore us.

Just what I wanted.

"I hear Gu'zod Alabest, the comedian, is on the space station," the Vessar said. He lifted his drink and took a sip.

Ah, was that the head of the operation? Amazing. I could track down Gu'zod and bribe someone in the group to spill the information I needed. Maybe I could wrap this up within a few dias and get home in time to spend the holidays at the orphanage where I was raised. My sister and her new mate told me they hoped to see me there. I'd bring presents to the younglings and visit with the Aunties who ran the place.

"Gu'zod," I said, faking a frown. "What planet is he from again?"

Finally, I might learn the species of the head of the smuggling operation.

He tapped his wrist com, and mine buzzed. A glance at mine showed nothing unusual. Maybe the buzz came from a local power surge.

My contact's arm dropped onto the table. "His family hails from many locations, but he was born . . ." He frowned down at his hand still lying on the book but was now twitching. "He was born . . ." His rheumy gaze met mine, and his tail spiked up, slicing through the back of his chair.

I rose and backed away, looking from the drink to him.

The Vessar gurgled and toppled backward, landing on the floor with a heavy thud.

A few patrons looked our way before turning back to their drinks or games. The bartender scowled in our direction.

I knelt down beside the Vessar, who stared at the ceiling. His breathing hitched, and foam oozed from the corner of his mouth. He was dying, and there wasn't anything I could do about it. Poisoned, most likely.

"Call a medic," I bellowed.

The bartender hurried around the counter, heading this way. "What's going on?"

"I'm sorry," I told him, placing a hand on his chest. "We'll get help."

"Too . . . late." He gurgled, his eyes widening.

Fuck. We all took risks in this job and many of us paid the final price.

He shoved a silver disc about half the length of my finger into my hand.

I pocketed it and leaned close to him. "Hang in there. Help is coming."

"Leader," he said in a strangled, wispy voice. "Leader is . . ."

I leaned nearer, waiting . . .

"Leader is Ergeepelon." His eyes rolled back in his head, and his breath shuddered out. He didn't inhale again.

Rising, I backed away.

"What did you do to him?" the bartender asked, pointing her pistol at my head. "Vessars don't like when one of their pack turns up dead."

"Indigestion," I said, easing toward the door. She couldn't call the authorities as there were none. Gangs on the space station policed themselves. But she might notify the head of the local Vessar pack. The lizard mafia was known throughout the galaxies for their thirst for vengeance. "He said something about his belly being upset."

"Why's he lying on the floor, then?" she asked with a twist of her lips. The gun started to lower, though she kept her hand on the switch.

I shrugged, still slipping toward the door. Almost halfway. "Sleeping. He had a rough night."

When her attention stopped pinning me to the wall, and she started toward the corner, I raced for the door.

Bellows rang outside, followed by a yelp of pain.

I'd know that voice anywhere.

Tatum.

I barreled through the door and around the side, aiming for the dumpster.

Tatum stood in front of it, brandishing his knife while three Poosines tried to grab him.

Snuggles stood beside Tatum, hissing and snarling, but the Poosines would ignore my pet. He was vicious, but he couldn't do much damage to their leathery hides.

A fourth Poosine was crawling along the upper wall, trying to get behind Tatum. They'd grab him, and I'd never see him again, something I should almost welcome. For whatever reason, the thought hit me in the guts like the kick of a ravalest.

I cared about the youngling whether I wanted to or not. No way would I let a nest of Poosines take him.

Pulling two blades from sheaths at my waist, I ran toward them, snarling.

One glanced over its shoulder and dismissed me. Tatum was their prey, and the creature must assume they could take him and still evade me.

I leapt, slicing out as I passed them, severing a head.

The Poosine crawling along the wall dropped onto my back, knocking us both to the slimy ground. I rolled, taking the heavy creature with me, gouging out with my blades. I got lucky, the tip of my knife eviscerating the creature. It went limp, and I tossed it off me, jumping to my feet.

The remaining Poosines were dragging Tatum out of the alley while he bellowed and squirmed. If they reached the market, they'd hide within the crowd. I wouldn't be able to track them.

I scrambled after them, my lungs on fire and my heart pounding like thunder. As they reached the head of the alley, I flung myself at them, knocking one Poosine against the side of the bar and the other to the ground.

I landed hard on top of Tatum and rolled, taking him with me.

The Poosines, seeing I wasn't going to give up, scrambled to their many limbs and fled, merging into the market beyond the alley.

Tatum lay beneath me, his gaze meeting mine. My hand lay on his chest, over a soft, round mound. A nipple peaked from my touch, and Tatum's eyes widened.

Tatum was not a youngling boy.

He was a mature female.

CHAPTER NINE
TATUM

I shrieked, smacking Matis's arm. "Get your meaty hand off my . . ."

"Breast?"

The word seemed to echo around us, though his voice came out barely above a whisper.

"I don't have breasts."

"Then what's this?" He massaged my boob, and my stupid nipple perked up and shouted hip hip hooray.

I bucked but couldn't dislodge him. "Stop groping me."

"Some females like it."

"I'm not some females."

A flick of his hand, and he pressed a blood-stained knife against my throat. "Who are you? *What* are you?"

I deflated, collapsing against the slimy ground. "I'm Tatum. I already told you that."

"Why did you let me think you were male?"

"Would you saunter around showing off your boobs in a seedy space station?"

"Not unless I was selling them by the horus."

My lips thinned. "Something I don't do. Nothing wrong with it, but it's not for me." Actually, I was a virgin, but I wasn't announcing that to a snarly Matis. "When I snuck on board, I needed to hide. I told you that already."

He sheathed his knife and lay there on me as if I was his squishy bed and he was settling in for a nice long nap.

Until a laser beam hit the wall beside his head.

Scrambling off me, he hauled me to my feet, tossed me over his shoulder, and bolted down the alley, scooping up Snuggles as he raced past the dumpster.

"Put me down," I cried, my belly lurching from being jarred against his shoulder.

Snuggles hissed at me. Nothing new there.

"I protected you back there, beast, in case you've forgotten," I snarled at the pet.

More laser beams hit the ground around us, scattering zistarns and making anyone lurking in the alley shrink into the shadows.

"What did you do in that bar?" I asked.

"What makes you think I did anything?"

"Because they're trying to kill you." I ducked and a beam shot over my head, taking a chunk off Matis's ear. The small cut didn't bleed. Laser cauterized. One of the issues with laser cuts was that they sometimes fused the wrong parts together. You might survive a hit to a limb.

Your heart? Not a good time for anyone, even those with more than one heart.

A whine rang out, and Matis darted to the left, barely avoiding being impaled with a hatchet. I blinked as it quivered in the wall.

"Stop," someone cried. "Or we'll rip you to shreds with laser beams."

"Already trying to do that," Matis snarled, his boots smacking on the ground.

"Who's chasing us?" I squinted down the alley, but the lighting was too poor to see.

"I seem to have irritated a Vessar pack."

Shit. "Put me down. I'm not playing with the lizard mafia." They'd make me disappear. And before they did that, they'd make me wish I could disappear.

A fence stretched across the end of the long alley.

"Let me go," I said again. "Then I can crawl over the fence with you."

"No need," he said, leaping over the structure as if it was a puddle, not something eight feet tall.

"You can't carry me forever," I shouted.

He darted right and wove through a series of short streets, each grittier than the last. Finally, he slid around a corner and ducked into an arched entrance to a broken-down building.

He lifted his wrist com. "Firoh. Prepare for a quick departure." A frown filled his face. "Firoh?"

No reply.

"Fuck," he said. "They scrambled my com somehow."

I squirmed. "Put me down."

"I will once we're safe."

"There's no safety here. Let me go. I'll remain with you. I won't run. Promise."

He studied my face. "I just told you a Vessar pack is after me, and you're saying you'll stay with me? They're not after you."

"So I'm a sucker for other people. Or you're stuck with me." I wiggled again, and he lowered me to my feet, keeping a tight grip on my arm. "You're right. I should be running away, putting as much distance between us as I can." Somehow, my reason for being here had morphed into more than obtaining the statue.

Damn, I wasn't starting to fall for Matis, wasn't I?

"Why aren't you?" he asked, his probing gaze locking on mine.

Explaining meant revealing things about myself, and I didn't just mean my mom and the assignment. Feelings for Matis swarmed through me when I'd rather they didn't. "Why hasn't Firoh responded to your hail?" I asked to change the subject.

The distraction worked. Matis peered in the direction we'd come from, his laser pistol lifted. "I don't know."

"Does your ship have a beam?"

"Yes. If I can reach him, he can move us on board, and we'll get out of here."

"What if your cargo isn't loaded yet?"

"Our skins are worth more than any cargo."

"I imagine it's hard to make a living as a pirate if you pay for cargo, then leave it behind."

He grumbled. "It's hard to sell cargo if you're dead."

"And it's hard to escape here if you can't reach anyone to beam you to your ship."

Snuggles, as if disgusted with our ongoing bickering, jumped off Matis's shoulder and slunk to the edge of the doorway, poking his head out.

Matis ripped off his eye patch and stuffed it into his pocket. He squinted to our right where squatters had taken over the street, stretching coverings from one building to another and erecting crude shacks beneath. "Don't worry. I've got a plan."

"That's what I'm worried about."

"Don't think I've forgotten you're a female, *Tatum*."

"It's my real name." I shrugged. "Why does it matter? I'll still be your cabin . . . whatever. No one else needs to know."

He turned me, pinning me to the door. "I know."

"So don't strut around naked any longer."

"You . . ." Complete puzzlement filled his face. "You were watching me last night. Staring at my cock."

"Don't get too full of yourself, there, Matty."

"I suspect your ogling meant you wanted to share my bed."

"In your dreams." I rolled my eyes, forcing mockery into my voice. It was surprisingly hard because I had gaped at his cock last night.

But I didn't want to share his bed.

He leaned closer, and my stupid body inched forward to meet him.

"How old are you?" he grated out. I swore his attention was focused on my mouth.

"Twenty-eight."

"*Not* sixteen."

"I haven't been a teenager for a very long time."

I didn't expect him to kiss me.

But he did.

I should shove him away.

Instead, I wrapped my arms around him, pulling him fully against me.

CHAPTER TEN
MATIS

I couldn't believe I was kissing my cabin boy—girl —*woman*. I'd meant to say something mocking to continue to taunt her, but my gaze was drawn to her lips. When they parted, I couldn't resist.

She tasted sweet. Like pure perfection.

Her arms went around me. She didn't shove me away.

When she moaned and thrust her hips against me, I lifted her up, pressing her against the door.

My cock was aflame, surging up in my pants. Totally wrong for the situation, because the Vessars were hunting us, but I couldn't drag my mouth away from hers.

Shouts rang out in the distance, and I still couldn't stop grinding my cock against the crease between her legs long enough to see if the Vessars were surging down the alley. For all I knew, the entire space station was looking for me now.

She spread her legs wider, and each time I thrust forward, she met me, rubbing herself against me.

Her hands clutched my shoulders, her fingertips biting in. It felt heady, almost as good as the feel of her shifting her pussy against my cock.

I ripped my mouth off hers, my back spasming from my contorted position. But nothing could keep me from pushing my body against hers rhythmically.

Our gazes locked, and I read defiance mixed with lust in hers. If she told me to stop, I would in a flash, but she just rubbed harder, her breathing ragged and her fingers tightening on my skin.

Her head tipped back against the door, and her eyelashes—those long, thick eyelashes that had caught my attention and held it—fluttered. She pushed harder, moans ripping up her throat.

My cock was a steel pole in my pants, and each time I pumped it up between her legs, her body rippled, shuddered.

"Yes," she breathed, swallowing hard. "More. Hard. Faster!"

Nothing and no one could hold me back. I pushed against her, giving her everything she needed.

I felt her quivering down there before the movement took over her body.

Her gaze returned to mine, and for one instant, as heat shot up through my cock, her eyes softened.

We held each other as we succumbed to pleasure.

CHAPTER ELEVEN
TATUM

Well, that shouldn't have happened. He hadn't stuck his cock inside me, so I supposed I was still—mostly—a virgin.

I rested my forehead against his chest, breathing fast while my body stopped quivering and returned to the space station.

I slid my legs across his delectable ass and thick thighs, and he released me so I could find my footing.

He stepped back, though he remained inside the deep doorway.

Snuggles slunk back into the small area as if he'd been too disgusted to remain with us while we humped each other.

I wasn't prudish. My virginity had remained intact because I hadn't met a person I cared enough to toss it aside for.

I'd found immense satisfaction with Matis, but if he peeled off my clothing and plunged his thick cock inside me, I'd welcome him with open arms and legs. This was a bad thing. I had a feeling he could creep into my heart easily, and he'd squish it if I wasn't careful.

"That didn't happen," I said, my voice completely devoid of the spunk I needed to make my words stick. My body still hummed, and I worried if he tugged me into his arms and started kissing me again, I'd climb all over him for a second round.

One eyebrow lifting, he glanced down at the front of his pants, where his cock no longer slammed against the fabric. "Yet it did."

"Then it won't happen again."

His eyebrow remained notched. "So you say."

"So I *insist.*"

"I'm not going to fuck you for the first time out in public."

That wasn't reassuring. "You're not going to fuck me at all."

He backed me against the door again and leaned in close to whisper in my ear. "Is that a challenge, cabin *boy?*"

My arms had somehow found their way around his shoulders, and I fisted his hair as if I didn't want to release him. I nearly begged him to take things further before I bit back the words.

Snarling, I nudged him away.

He chuckled and hefted Snuggles, dropping his pet onto his shoulder. While the creature watched me, Matis poked his head out of the doorway, peering around. He put his eye patch back on.

"What's your plan to get us to your ship?" I asked, smoothing my clothing. "I assume they know who you are, and they'll be watching the ship."

"That's my assumption as well. The thing is, even if I can reach my ship, I don't want to leave the space station. Not yet."

"You said the lizard mafia is after you." If it was me, I'd already be on an outbound craft. Vessars didn't play; they devoured.

He shrugged, still looking around. "Just one pack."

"A pack's, what, fifty or so lizards?"

"More like a hundred."

I scoffed. "And you plan to take them on by yourself?"

He shot me a grin. "I'm not alone. I've got you."

That was the problem. He sort of did have me, and not just because I was still his cabin . . . person.

"What did you do in such a short time to incite a Vessar pack?" I asked, truly curious.

"They think I murdered one of them."

"Did you?" I squinted in the direction we'd come from, but other than a few aliens striding this way or that—and not looking in our direction—I didn't see anyone giving chase. Maybe we'd lost them.

"No."

"I assume the friend you came here to meet is lying dead in the bar," I said.

He shot me a grim look. "I'm going to take down whoever did it."

"Do you happen to have a name for the true murderer?"

"No, but he's Ergeepelon."

Funny, so was the alien who'd sent me on this assignment. I should mention that, but how could I share the details with Matis? He wouldn't open his safe and hand me the artifact without questions I wasn't prepared to answer.

If I didn't complete the job, I wouldn't have the funds to save my mom.

A different Ergeepelon must be after him.

"There are a lot of Ergeepelons on the space station," I said. "I saw a bunch of them as we made our way to the bar."

"I have a feeling we're going to find out how many there truly are on this space station." Matis took my hand, which was a nice change from gripping my upper arm and pulled me out of the doorway.

He darted to the right with me following, leaping over aliens sleeping in the street and others sitting, their gazes glazed after taking altered brugeer. The drug made Vessars act silly, but some species laced it with chemicals that enhanced the brugeer effect enough to get them high.

Shouts echoed in the alleys we'd traveled, but I didn't sense they'd seen us—yet.

Matis took us through a series of dingy streets, and I soon lost my sense of direction. He stopped at the end of an alley, peering out.

A variety of aliens lumbered and strode past us, and in the distance, some called out, selling their wares. Since the street was narrow, this must be a local market, independent from the big one we'd passed through earlier.

"All clear," he hissed, rushing forward, still leading me with a hand tight around mine. I sensed he didn't want to let me go, though I wasn't sure why. He didn't need a cabin boy enough to keep me around. Barely armed, I was a handicap. He already knew I couldn't fight, and that I had secrets. It would be easier to hide without me tagging along.

Snuggles blinked at me, and while I didn't see hatred in his cat-like eyes, I didn't find acceptance.

Because I wanted to see how he'd respond, I reached up and stroked the pet's spine. For a secunda, he leaned into my hand before he realized it was me and not Matis touching him. He scrambled over to Matis's other shoulder and shot me a dark look.

At least he wasn't trying to rip my hand off.

Matis continued to watch the street, but none of the aliens gave us more than a cursory glance.

"Why aren't you ditching me?" I asked.

He squinted down at me. "Why would I do that?"

"You don't care about me."

A tic bloomed on his brow, and his jaw tightened. "And what makes you think that?"

"Feelings, Matis?" I scoffed, though I watched him like a jarvan.

"I care about others," he said.

"A generic answer."

He reeled around to face me, watching me. Did he think my expression would give something away? "Are you suggesting what we just did meant nothing to you?"

"Should it?" I shrugged, but I wasn't brushing him off.

He huffed. "Perhaps not to you, but it did to me. You . . ." He dragged his palms across the top of his head. "I hired you. I thought . . ."

I tilted my head, watching him. "What?"

"You reminded me of myself when I was a youngling."

"Did you sneak on board a pirate spaceship and stab someone? You give the impression death waits for those who tangle with you, but I sense you're squishy inside."

"I am."

He'd reveal it just like that, huh? "I'd think your reputation would make you deny it."

He stroked Snuggles. "There's nothing wrong with caring for others. Maybe you should try it sometime."

I did care for others—my mom, anyway. But he made a valid point. I'd shied away from everyone else.

Earth had changed a lot since I was little. Overrun with all sorts of aliens and the creatures they brought and set free; people couldn't freely walk down a street without endangering their lives.

I'd learned to blend in, and I'd learned to hide my heart to keep from being hurt. Even now, I protected myself from the imminent death of my mother by running away. Well, not quite running. I needed credits to cure her, but maybe I should've remained on Earth and found a different way to do it.

"Floundering in self-reflection?" he asked.

I lifted my chin. "Why would you think that?"

He grinned. "Because you *are* a bit like me, and that's what I'd be doing."

"I'm female. An Earthling."

Turning back to the entrance to the alley, he spoke over his shoulder. "You're still like me."

I huffed, not sure of that.

He tugged me from the alley, leading me through crowds of aliens from more species than I'd ever found on Earth.

Ahead, a sign with the portrait of a multi-breasted, blue-skinned alien female swayed in the light breeze swirling through the space station. No outside wind made its way to the board, but compressors ran everywhere, maintaining temperature and filtering the air. They generated the gust I periodically felt on my face.

Matis stopped beneath the sign and took in a deep breath, releasing it. He hustled me forward, and we stepped into the establishment.

The heavy scent of flowers and tinny music greeted us. Males and females of various species lounged on furniture upholstered in red and gold velvet. Brugeer smoke coated the air, making me sneeze.

None of the patrons looked our way, being too busy with whoever was lounging on top of them or squatting in front of them with their legs spread wide.

"Jeez, Matis," I said. "You brought me to an interstellar brothel?"

"Where better to hide?" he said with a teasing grin.

"Ah, Matis," someone said in a voice silkier than cloutine. A four-armed, blue-skinned alien female as tall as Matis sauntered toward him, her hips swaying in time to the music. She stopped in front of him, meeting his eye and completely ignoring me. I recognized her from the sign. "I didn't think I'd see you here again."

"Yet, here I am," he said with a cocky grin that made my skin prickle with irritation. "How are you doing, Isirana?"

Her palm snapped across his face.

CHAPTER TWELVE
MATIS

"Now, Isirana," I said, holding my body steady despite her blow. Yeah, it stung, but I'd expected it. After all, I'd skipped out the last time I was here without saying goodbye. Never mind that three yaros had passed since then. Isirana never forgot a slight. "Is that how you treat a friend?"

"How dare you come here?" she snarled, her four breasts heaving with her outrage.

"Would it help if I said I missed you?" I said.

She huffed. Reaching out, she stroked Snuggles, who purred and leaned into her touch. "At least my little boompkins is glad to see me." Spying Tatum, she leaned around me, her two smiles slyly creasing her face. "Now, who might you be? A youngling come to pop something he no longer needs?"

Now that I knew Tatum twas female, I couldn't understand how in the galaxies everyone else didn't realize she wasn't male. The evidence didn't just lie in her pretty face and long lashes, but in the curves she tried to hide with loose clothing.

"Hi," Tatum mumbled, bobbing her head. "I'm Tatum."

"Perhaps you'd like to come with me, then, Tatum," Isirana said in a sultry voice. "I promise a wonderful time." Her face hardened when she looked at me. "You can wait out on the street." Her hands fluttered toward the door. "Go. Go!"

"I'm remaining inside." I latched onto Tatum's hand. "And he stays with me."

"I didn't think you traveled in that direction," Isirana said. "But what do I know? I learned quite quickly that you're not the male I believed you to be."

"This your girlfriend?" Tatum asked, gesturing to Isirana.

"Yes," Isirana said at the same time I half-shouted *no*.

Tatum grumbled and shot me a look of disgust. "I can wait here while you two . . . get reacquainted."

"I've moved on from this measly male," Isirana said. She pointed to the door. "I asked you to leave, Matis. Do not return to my business again."

Bellows rang out on the street, and multiple footsteps stomped by. I eased us away from the clear plexi panel on the door.

"Could we stay here for a bit?" I asked in a placating tone, holding my palm out to Isirana.

She sniffed, ignoring my hand. "In trouble, are you?"

"Something like that," I said.

"I should notify the authorities you're here, then," she added with a slick grin.

I pulled a sack of credits from my pocket and held it out. "Perhaps you can be persuaded to delay notification for a while?"

Her double lips pouted, and she clutched all four of her hands to her sizeable chest. "You suggest I can be bribed?" Fake tears dripped from her eyes and her silver, living hair drifted out from her head.

I added another, smaller bag to the first.

She snatched them up and pivoted on her pointy heels. "Follow me. You'll have to room with the youngling; business has been lively lately."

Nodding to Tatum, I urged him to follow Isirana while I peeked through the clear plexi, onto the street. Vessars roamed the area, hefting those sleeping on the ground to study their faces before tossing them aside and digging through a dumpster.

They wouldn't give up easily.

I strode across the room, following Isirana and Tatum. At the back, Isirana sauntered up the red-carpeted stairs to a landing. A hall with doors on either side stretched in both directions. She took a right, and at the end, placed her fingertip on a small panel beside the door.

"You too," she told me, and I coded it to my touch.

The door opened, and we stepped inside.

"Can we get some food?" I asked.

Isirana held out her hand.

I gave her a few credits.

She stared at them for a secunda, her lips twisting, before sighing and turning to sway down the hall. "I'll send something up."

"Water for a bath too," I called out.

Isirana lifted one arm.

After ensuring the door was locked, I put Snuggles on the floor to prowl and leaned against the back of the door.

"A bath, Matis?" Tatum asked.

"I like to be clean. You need to bathe yourself unless you plan to sleep on the floor."

She grumbled, taking in the narrow bed, the solitary window on one wall looking out at yet another dingy alley, and the simple rug on the floor. "Not very seductive for a bordello, is it?"

"People come here for one thing only. The ambiance downstairs lures them in, but up here, most don't bother to turn on a light."

"How about you?" she asked, her posture tight.

"There's something to be said for watching a female's face while you give her pleasure."

Color rose in her cheeks, and she whirled away from me, striding to the window to look out.

"I haven't been here for yaros," I said. "Which is why Isirana is angry with me." For some reason, I wanted Tatum to understand I hadn't been with anyone in a long time, that what we'd done was special. That I wanted more. But she was skittish enough already. I worried she'd bolt, so I'd keep the information to myself until I was more confident of a welcoming reception.

"Then Isirana *was* your girlfriend," she bit out, pacing the small room.

I shrugged. "We had an agreement of sorts."

A snarl ripped from her throat. "You fucked her, in other words."

"I doubt she was exclusive. That's not Isirana."

"What about you? Did you have feelings for her?"

Snuggles watched, his head snapping back and forth between us.

Why did Tatum sound pissed off about this? It wasn't like she and I . . .

Oh.

"You're jealous," I said, trying not to crow about it.

"I am not jealous," she bit out, her little hands forming fists at her sides as she stormed over to stand in front of me.

I'd been smacked once today and didn't care for a repeat, so I eased around her.

"It's okay if you are," I said. "I'll be honest with you. I'm self-aware enough to know I felt the beginnings of attraction for Tatum, the cabin boy. I'm grateful you're older than I thought and *not* a boy."

"There can't be anything between us," she said, deflating.

Why had my comment knocked the wind out of her? "*Can't* is an interesting term."

"Won't, then." She backed away, slumping onto the bed. Did she note how close she'd landed to Snuggles and how my pet was peering at her with interest and not irritation? I assumed not when she leaned back on her palms, ignoring him.

Snuggles sniffed her hand before curling up nearby.

"If you're worried about the boss-employee thing," I said. "Consider yourself my companion."

"Like your mistress?" she sputtered.

"An old-fashioned term, but sure, if you're interested in that role." While it should be too soon to think about her and me and a future, I kept picturing us together. It wouldn't be the first time two pirates were intimate and co-captained a ship. And if . . . This was thinking *way* far ahead. But if we progressed, I'd have to eventually tell her what I really did for a living.

"If you want a good fuck," she said, "I'm sure Isirana's hurt feelings can be soothed."

I stalked over to the bed and braced myself over her. "What if I don't want Isirana?"

She sucked in a breath and leaned away until she lay flat on the bed with her legs dangling over the side. Her gaze landed on my mouth and her cute little tongue poked out to glide across her lower lip.

My cock shot upright, knocking on my pants to be let out.

"There might be, um," she swallowed hard, "other females here who'd catch your eye."

"And what if I want you, Tatum?"

She slithered out from beneath me and leapt to her feet, backing all the way to the door. "I . . ."

Someone banged on the panel. "Food! Water!"

With relief on her face, she turned and opened the door. Three young male Wurmars entered, one carrying a tray with our meal, plus drying cloths tucked beneath his arm. He laid the tray on a table and tossed the cloths on the bed, pivoting and leaving without making eye contact.

Another Wurmar carried in a metal tub, and the third was laden with buckets. Once the tub had been placed on one side, the second Wurmar dumped in the water.

"More come," he said, striding through the open doorway.

Much of the space station had higher tech, including cleansing units one could step inside and emerge clean. Other parts chugged along the way they had for generations. While there was a small chamber attached to this room with a toilet and a cleansing unit, Isirana understood me well enough to know I preferred bathing in real water.

Once the tub was full, the Wurmars retreated to the hall.

I closed and locked the door.

"So, little human," I said, crossing my arms over my chest. "Will we eat or should we take a bath together first?"

CHAPTER THIRTEEN

TATUM

I felt like I'd been sucked into a black hole and spit out in an alternate reality.

He wanted to bathe together, did he? I fumed, my facing getting hot. If he thought I'd—

Matis watched me with a smirk on his face. He knew what I was thinking. He knew I'd storm around and snarl at him.

Two could play this game.

"We *should* bathe first," I said calmly. I tugged my shirt over my head and tossed it aside. "Is there a sanitizer I could use to clean my clothing?" I stepped toward him and lifted his chin that had dropped—though I almost had to jump up to do it. He gaped at the binder I'd wrapped around my breasts. I wasn't small there, and my flesh oozed around the cloth.

"I, um . . . I." He glanced toward a small unit sitting on a corner shelf.

"Good," I said. I unclipped the fastener to my binder

and slowly unwound it. My breasts sprung free from the constraint, my nipples rosy and beaded from the friction. Or so I told myself. Heat swirled inside me, and the flames licked down to touch between my legs. I couldn't stop thinking about what we'd done in the doorway and how I might like to do something similar again.

Sure, I was irritated he'd been with Isirana, but how could I complain about it when we hadn't known each other? This was different, right? Damn, I hoped so.

Should I tell him I was a virgin?

I wasn't sure it mattered. I was in control of this, and if I didn't want to take things all the way, I wouldn't.

The thought of losing my V-Card to an alien pirate titillated me, though whatever we did would be much more than that. He said he was attracted to me almost from the start. I was drawn to him immediately. Well, after I stabbed him. We'd fumed at each other, but instead of repelling me, our squabbling made me ache for his touch.

Snuggles took one look at me and hopped off the bed, slinking into the tiny attached room containing a toilet.

Matis's jaw kept dropping, and he was breathing faster than he'd done when we raced through the streets.

I was such a tease.

I stood boldly in front of him, savoring his appreciative gaze gliding down my body like a heavy caress. His hand lifted toward my breasts, but I backed away. I wasn't quite ready to give everything to him. He was too full of himself to step into his arms and let him do whatever he wanted with me.

What future could I have with a space pirate?

I shimmied out of my pants and underwear. With way more boldness than I possessed, I turned away from him and sauntered over to the sanitizer, chucking my clothing inside and engaging the device. It would clean and fold it, and I could put everything back on after my bath.

Ignoring his heavy breathing, I stepped into the tub and leaned back against the side. It was big, but it was going to be a tight squeeze with both me and Matis.

Slitting one eye his way, I frowned. He stood where I'd left him, his eyes wide and a sizeable bulge pressing against the front of his pants.

"You . . ." he said.

"You seem to have lost your train of thought, Matis," I said, savoring him fumbling for once. He had a ton of confidence, though I'd already seen it was well-earned. It was nice to surprise him.

"You took your clothing off," he said.

"As you so kindly pointed out, it was dirty."

"You're naked, in the tub."

My grin kept trying to blaze, but I suppressed it. I was having so much fun! "That I am, oh, pirate captain."

He blinked a minue before his face smoothed. As I'd assumed, he recovered and strode over to stand beside the tub, staring down at my body beneath the water. A tic sprung up on his brow.

His cock rocked against his pants.

How far did I want to take this? Teasing was one

thing, but I didn't want to hold something out then snatch it away. I might be cautious, but I wasn't a jerk.

I'd never done anything like this with another person.

"Are you going to watch or take a bath?" I asked. Noting a bar of soap on a nearby shelf, plus a scrap of cloth, so I started lathering up.

His eyes widened again when I ran the soapy cloth over my neck, but he pretty much drooled when I dipped it beneath the water and across my breasts.

I ducked down beneath the water and wet my hair, soaping it up. Like him, I enjoyed being clean. I'd only contemplated wearing the same things over and over because they were all I had and they covered up my identity.

After rinsing my hair, I washed my belly and legs. Each stroke heated me up further. It was a wonder the water wasn't boiling.

When I ran the cloth between my legs, Matis gulped.

His pants outlined his cock. It was big and thick—not that I had any personal experience to gauge cock size. But I watched vids. I'd seen cocks in many colors and with various titillating components. Was Matis's as copper as the rest of him? Did he have a spur or nubs along the sides?

Despite my lack of cock experience, I knew what to expect if we did it. And I knew what my body liked. Right now, it craved Matis.

After my feet were clean, I wrung out the cloth and held it out to him. He stared down at it blankly.

"Wash my back?" I asked.

"Yes. I'd be happy to." He took the cloth and went around behind me, stooping down to rub along my spine. Each stroke drove my body higher. He'd barely have to touch me to get me off. My clit throbbed, and my nipples ached to be sucked.

He tossed the cloth onto the floor with a wet smack, and his hands landed on my shoulders. "You . . ."

"Me?" I peered up at him.

"Make room in that tub, little human." He straightened and tossed aside his shirt, shucking his pants quickly after.

His cock pressed against his ripped abs, a long, thick thing with a life of its own. If he had a spur on the top, I couldn't see it. But I did spy nubs along the sides, plus an intriguing head that was a bit thicker than his length.

He stood at the side of the tub. "All or nothing, Tatum?"

"What do you mean by that?" I asked, my voice as breathy as if I'd run for hours.

"Once I'm in that water, you're mine to do whatever I please with." When I blinked at his words and sputtered, his bark cut through. "All or nothing?"

I swallowed. "I, um, haven't gone all the way with anyone."

"You're saying you're a virgin?"

I nodded.

"Very well."

His words didn't tell me what he thought about my admission, but I wanted to know.

Silly me for thinking I was in control of this situation.
"All or nothing?" he said again.
Now or never, right?
"All," I whispered.
"Good girl."

CHAPTER FOURTEEN
MATIS

I stepped into the tub and settled down across from her, placing my legs on either side of her thighs.

A virgin. Some guys loved taking a female for the first time. Others preferred being with someone with experience.

My only thought was to make sure Tatum enjoyed this as much as she should. This was more than about me and the needs of my body.

My emotions were already involved. Did I love her? It was hard to know something like that after such a short period of time.

But I could.

My protective instincts were triggered the minue I met her. They'd only heightened since. We were in deep shit, but I still enjoyed being with her. Her snarky mouth triggered heat deep inside me. I sensed she always would.

"Why?" I asked.

"Why what?" She clutched the soap to her chest.

"You're twenty-eight. Why still a virgin and why decide to hand it over to me?"

"It never felt like the right time, and don't start thinking this means anything just because we're going to do it."

There was the snarly female I'd come to adore. "It *does* mean something."

"I've pleasured myself. I doubt there's a scrap of hymen left to pop, but if it makes your chest puff, you can crow afterward."

"It has nothing to do with that, though we'll get back to you pleasuring yourself in due time." Damn, I wanted to watch. Would she let me? It took trust, and we weren't there yet. Funny how I suspected we'd get there eventually.

I really was falling for her, and instead of being scared, I welcomed it. It felt like the right time and the right person even if we were in considerable danger.

"You don't need to share if you don't want to," I said. No need to push her for answers. "Virginity is special to a lot of people."

"What about you?"

I snorted. "Lost that a long time ago."

Her eyebrows lifted, and she placed the soap on the shelf, relaxing her hands at her sides. "Here?"

"At the orphanage where I grew up. I was sixteen and too young for anything like that."

"Sixteen *is* young, though you probably didn't feel too young back then."

"She was eighteen and seemed incredibly worldly to me. We fumbled around, and I doubt either of us enjoyed it much."

Her nose twisted. "I'm sure you did. You got off, right?"

"Too quickly. However, I wasn't *that* unworldly. I made sure she found some pleasure in most of it even if it didn't come from my cock."

"That's good of you."

I shrugged. "Despite what you might think, I'm a decent person."

"For a pirate."

"Yup." I wanted to tell her what I really did for a living, but I knew so little about her.

"Tell me more about growing up in an orphanage," she said, watching me with curiosity; not fear.

"Are you saying you don't want me to have sex with you right away?"

"Foreplay's a thing, Matis."

"Oh, I'm very good at that."

"So says the guy who admits he fumbled around before finally giving a female a bit of pleasure, though not with his cock."

Touché. "That was sixteen yaros ago. I've learned a few tricks since then."

"From Isirana."

I shrugged. "I'm no gossip."

"Back to the orphanage."

"The ladies who run it are amazing. My family was killed during the Evarian-Human War."

"You're not Evarian or human," she said. Her toes tickled my inner thighs, and I liked it. She was so much tinier than me. Would my cock fit?

"I'm Dralian," I said.

"Some call your species ogres."

I shrugged. It wasn't a slur. Humans had their own mythology, and Dralians looked much like their fictious ogres. "The Evarians raided my planet. My family was caught up in it."

"How old were you?" Sympathy softened her voice.

"It doesn't matter."

"Maybe it does, but you don't need to share." An edge of sharpness had returned to her voice. Did she realize it gave her away? Some of her emotions were wrapped up in me.

I liked that. I could work with it.

Because I wasn't giving up.

I wanted her, and I was going to claim everything she had to offer.

CHAPTER FIFTEEN

TATUM

"I was five-yaros-old when my family was killed," Matis said, his voice devoid of emotion. But his gorgeous eyes told me the true story. He still hurt; the memory would haunt him forever.

A tiny part of him was still the little kid who'd lost his world.

"I'm sorry."

"It happened. You're not responsible."

"Every kid should be raised by people who love them."

"I did. The ladies at the orphanage are amazing. Every youngling growing up there feels like they matter. They make sure each of us not only has a home and are fed and clothed, but that we feel special."

"I'm glad you were given that chance."

"What about you?" he asked. "Did the war impact you?"

"My dad was killed in battle. My mom . . . She wasn't."

"I'm sorry about your dad."

"Thanks. I had Mom, and that made a difference."

Poor Matis, losing everyone he loved. Whatever irritation I'd been building inside me burst, leaving only sympathy behind. Plus emotions I wasn't sure how to define or handle.

He was a ruthless pirate. An irritating, ruthless pirate. I should climb out of the tub and run away. I could find a new way to help my mom.

But I couldn't leave and not only because my body ached for something it had never tasted before. Like I said, I could pleasure myself, so it wasn't about that.

I wanted to do it with him, and not just have sex. I wanted to fall apart in his arms and see the same feeling echoed in him.

I liked him more than I should. I'd been sent to steal something from him, and if we were going to have anything more between us, I needed to confess and quit the job I was hired to do. I'd then lose any chance to help my mom, but the thought of betraying Matis hurt almost as much. How had my life become so complicated? I didn't have time for emotions or him.

Yet, here I was, sitting in a cooling tub, chatting about his past, learning about what made him tick.

Falling for him despite my determination to keep my heart separate from this encounter.

Could I be with him without my soul getting involved?

"What are you thinking?" he asked. "Having second thoughts?" Did I hear a hint of vulnerability in his voice?

I could reply in a snarky manner. Crawl all over him and distract him with the lust I still saw simmering in his eyes. But I didn't want to do that.

Curse me, I wanted to create something lasting and special with him, and not just because he'd be my first. I hadn't been completely honest with him in many ways, even when it came to what we were about to do. I'd never given anyone my body, because I'd never cared enough to offer it.

Falling for someone meant taking a risk. I'd lost my dad, and my mom hovered close to death. I was wise enough to know I protected my heart—and by extension, my body—to keep from being hurt.

Maybe this once, I could give someone my trust. I could let fate decide. If we were meant to be together, things would work out. If fate had something different in mind for us, at least I'd know I gave it a chance.

"I think we should stop talking and find another way to distract ourselves," I said, the farthest I dared release my emotions. Little steps before big ones.

"Did I take this in the wrong direction?" He winced. "Maybe you don't want emotions tied up in whatever we have."

"What *do* we have, Matis?" I held my breath, waiting for his answer.

He crawled up over me, bracing his palms on the rim of the tub on either side of my shoulders. Leaning close, he kept his voice low. "Now, if I told you, I'd probably scare you away."

"Maybe I can handle whatever you want to throw in my direction."

"What about this?" He placed his lips softly on mine, but he did nothing with them, as if he was testing the waters between us.

Even his light touch felt good.

I braced my palms on his shoulders and parted my lips.

Given permission, his tongued dipped inside to tangle with mine.

My heart split wide open, and my moan of desire slipped from deep inside me. I clung to him, moving my mouth beneath his, taking as much as I gave. Heat coiled tightly inside me; a wild thing that ached to be set free.

He traced his fingers down my neck and paused at the crest of my breast.

I lifted my chest toward him, needing his touch more than I'd needed anything else in my life.

This shouldn't be so wonderful. So untamed and visceral.

He kissed beneath my ear, then continued across my jaw, following the trail laid by his fingers. He slid a claw across my nipple, taking it between his fingertips and rolling it.

My groan was wrenched from deep inside me. Sure, I'd touched myself. I'd taken pleasure when I needed it. But there was something amazing about having someone else take the lead. I didn't know what he'd do next, and anticipation kept shooting through me, bolts of lightning that made the low simmer in my core blaze.

Lifting his head, he watched my face as he continued to stroke my breast. His knee slid between my thighs, parting me, opening me up for whatever came next.

For the first time, I wanted him to make me come instead of me taking care of things myself.

Matis. I wanted Matis.

He continued watching me as his fingers glided down my belly and between my legs.

"Tell me what you like," he said.

"Everything."

"This?" He ran a knuckle across my clit, parting me along the way.

I bucked my hips up and moaned.

"And this?" He slid his finger or knuckle or something inside me while another part of his hand centered on my clit, stroking it.

"Where are your claws?" I gasped, my eyes sliding shut. With them closed, I could focus solely on the sensations he was tugging from my body.

"Retractable. Handy, huh?"

"Oh, hell, yes."

"We've determined your sweet little clit likes attention." His voice came out all growly. I adored it. "What about this part of you?" He slid a finger deep inside me.

I groaned.

"Tell me how this makes you feel, Tatum. I need to know." He pulled his finger out and pushed it back inside, swirling it around to make sure each part of my inner walls got equal attention.

"It feels amazing. I like it."

"Just like, huh? How about this?" He pumped harder, faster.

I was a panting wreck already. When I did this for myself, I knew what I'd do next and how I'd feel during each step. Handing Matis complete control opened this up to a new adventure, one I worried would soon become addictive.

He pushed something thicker inside me, but it wasn't his cock. That was shifting against my lower thigh.

"You're incredibly tight," he grated out, his face creased with strain. "This is only two fingers. How does it feel?"

"Maybe I need a bigger dildo."

His lips quirked up, and his gaze met mine. "I think I can provide something big enough to satisfy."

I grinned. "I believe you can."

"Do two fingers feel okay?"

"You're making this technical, Matis." Humor bubbled up in my voice.

"Far be it for me to do that."

He pressed more inside me. Three fingers? My brain swirled away, stating it wasn't interested in analyzing the situation.

It only wanted to feel.

He pumped his fingers inside me while encircling my clit, driving me higher and higher.

A wreck already; I bucked up to meet each of his thrusts.

"Four," he grated out, pushing them inside me. "I'm worried, Tatum."

"Don't analyze," I barked.

"I'm freaking huge. Wider than four fingers."

"Stop it." I cupped his face, making him meet my gaze. "If you don't finish this . . . If you don't give me what I need, I'm going to traipse downstairs and hit Isirana up for a male to service me."

"Fuck, no," he growled. "I am not only going to satisfy you now, but I'm also going to make sure you come again during your first time with a cock."

"Promises, promises." How I found enough brain power to speak while he was finger fucking my pussy, I'll never know. "I need a delivery, Matis, not a notification of the order."

"You're incredibly naughty, love." He pulled his fingers out, my body sucking on them, the greedy thing that it was.

He clambered out of the tub and lifted me, striding over to the bed, where he tossed me on the blankets.

"We're making everything wet."

"You're not even close to wet enough, little human. But no worries," he climbed up over me, spreading my legs wide and dropping between them. "I'm gonna get you so wet, you'll be gushing."

CHAPTER SIXTEEN
MATIS

I couldn't believe I was here with Tatum doing this. But in so many ways, it felt right.

I suspected we were destined for each other, but I wasn't going to dwell on that thought for long. Not while I had her right where I wanted her: her legs splayed wide and moans rising up her throat.

As I glided my finger down her crease, I marveled at how wet she was. I'd already determined she was tight. Maybe too tight for what I had to offer, but we'd make this work. It was important that she find as much pleasure as possible from her first time, which was why I wasn't going to rush this. By the time I drove my cock inside her, she'd be so close to coming, it wouldn't take much to spill her over.

I pushed two fingers inside her while stroking her clit with the pad of my thumb. Her guttural breathing echoed in the room, driving me to take even more care with her precious body.

Licking up her slit, I teased it around my fingers I kept pumping, driving them deep within her as she rose to meet me. When I sucked on her clit, she released a sharp cry. Her body trembled, but she wasn't there yet.

Spying her breasts with their perky nipples, I stroked one with my free hand. I still couldn't get over the fact that I'd thought she was male. This was a glorious female; one I was beginning to crave like no other.

My heart kept surging up into my throat. This wasn't just about claiming her body or even making her come multiple times, I wanted to further the bond between us. Fates help me, but I was lost in her.

This was going to change everything, but instead of being angry, my heart welcomed this.

"Matis," she sighed, pumping up to meet my fingers while I rolled her nipple. "I . . ."

"What do you want?" I asked, and my question wasn't solely about this minue. I needed to know what she wanted from me later on this dia, tomorrow, and a lunar cycle from now.

It was too soon, but would there ever be a time like this one? I thought not.

"Everything. This. You." Her breath snorted out. "I can't believe I'm saying that. I want you, Matis. Now."

"Because of this?" I licked her clit and, because I couldn't resist, I drove my tongue inside her along with my fingers, savoring her taste and the way her groan wrenched from her chest.

She latched on to my hair, holding tight, and I looked

up, my gaze meeting hers. "I want you, Matis. Fates help me, but I do. Not just now."

While I could huff about her getting lost in the sensations generated by my mouth and fingers, a thrill shot through me. Maybe there was more to this than just this minue for both of us.

"You have me, Tatum. I mean that." I thrust three fingers into her and swirled my tongue across her clit. I could feel her body tensing, tightening as she rode each crest to the top. It made my heart sing and it heightened my determination to make this as pleasurable for her as possible.

I sucked on her clit, slowing the pace of my fingers to deep thrusts.

She bucked and clung to my hair, her eyes rolled back and her body tense. With a jerky cry, she let go, spiraling. Her body shuddered, and her passage sucked on my fingers. I plunged harder, driving her body to wrench everything she could out of this minue.

I glided my fingers in and out of her, licking up her juices as she came again.

She flopped back on the bed and moaned. "You're trying to make me crave you forever, aren't you?"

"Would you feel better if I told you yes and that I feel the same?" Pulling my fingers out of her, I licked them clean.

She studied my face. "Are you just saying that? Here I am, giving you my V-Card. Most guys would say almost anything to a woman to get inside her pants."

"Is that what you think I'm doing?"

Her gaze met mine, and she bit down hard on her lower lip. "I don't know, Matis."

I rose over her, bracing myself with one arm beside her while stroking down her slit, teasing her sensitive clit with each pass. It would be easy to push inside her, to claim my own orgasm, but I wanted her with me, urging me on with her fingernails digging into my shoulders and her cries of pleasure echoing in the room.

I needed her emotions fully engaged.

"What we have came on fast," I said.

She nodded. "I couldn't stop staring at you almost from the minue I met you."

"Same. And I cursed myself for being attracted to a youngling."

A smile teased across her lips. "Which you now know I'm not."

"We snapped and snarled at each other for a reason."

"Because you were being a jerk?" she quipped.

"Is this a jerkish move?" I slid a finger inside her, keeping the pad of my thumb on her engorged clit. Her passage twitched, and wetness bathed my finger. She was almost ready again. I couldn't wait to feel her spasming around my cock.

She moaned; a heady sound that made my cock stiffen even further. I'd ridden along the edge, nearly coming when she did and without a single touch of her fingers. That was how into this minue and her I was. I could find my own pleasure just by seeing her own spill across her face.

"That's not jerkish," she said. Her eyelids closed, and

she thrust her hips up to meet my fingers. "You're distracting me."

"From the conversation or from what I'm doing to your body?"

"Both."

I stilled my fingers, because I wasn't going to do something to push her into this if she truly wasn't ready for it. Sure, she'd said she wanted to lose her virginity with me, but maybe she'd changed her mind. What we'd already done would be enough. Sure, my cock would complain, but I wouldn't do anything unless she was as into it as me.

"I want to talk," I said. "But I also want to sink my cock into your wetness and ride you all night. You choose."

She stared into my eyes for a long while before cupping my face. "Cock."

With a grin, I placed one of her legs, then the other, around my waist.

I centered the thick head of my cock at her core, and after stroking it through her wetness, making sure I glided it over her clit each time, I drove my hips forward, pausing once I was inside to give her body time to adjust.

"Tight," she said, her eyes pinched closed. "It burns."

"I'll stop," I said, starting to pull out.

She latched onto my arms. "Do not stop. Get that thing inside me. Give my body a chance to adjust but do it."

I nodded, barely able to think. She felt so good, her

passage clinging to my cock. With a grunt, I pushed in farther.

"Yes," she said, her head thrashing on the pillow. "More."

"I don't want to hurt you."

"It's not. It feels good."

All right then. I hitched my hips forward, sinking my cock deep inside her.

CHAPTER SEVENTEEN

TATUM

I'd pleased myself with a variety of vibrators. Thick ones and ones with nubs that quivered until I shut them off. None of them could compare to the real thing.

Actually, nothing and no one could compare to Matis.

"Are you with me?" he asked in a guttural voice, his cock buried deep within me.

The stretch was almost more than I could take. I felt full all the way to my belly. Despite him using many fingers, he was still bigger. I'd seen it, though, so I knew what to expect.

Expectations paled when compared to the girth and length surging against my core.

"Tatum?" he growled. "Do I need to stop or . . .?"

"Why are you chatting?" I asked with a smile. I grabbed onto his hair and tugged. "You're all talk and no action." I was teasing, and I could tell he knew by how his eyes gleamed and the growl rumbling around in his chest.

"No action, huh?" he asked, rising to the challenge just like I hoped he would. He pulled out and pushed back inside me.

I could tell he was taking care not to hurt me, which I appreciated, but soon, I wanted him to let go. Seeing him come undone was the best thing that could ever happen.

For a virgin, my body was pleasingly accommodating. Just because a real cock hadn't been inside there didn't mean my pussy couldn't figure out how to handle it.

Owning a fleet of vibrators wasn't such a bad idea. However, I had a feeling I'd be throwing them out when I got home. They weren't big enough, nubbed enough, and they didn't have that . . .

"Shit. Spur," I cried as I pushed up to meet his thrusts. "Yay."

"You like it?" he gritted out, his face tight and the muscles of his arms and chest bulging as he rocked back and forth against me. Strain filled his face, and his muscles bulged in his chest and shoulders. He was barely holding himself together, and I loved it.

However, I wanted him to go wild.

"Stop being gentle," I said, yanking on his hair again. Because I didn't want to hurt him, I let go and grabbed onto his sides. He was so much taller than me. While connected, I was lip-level with his pecs.

"What do you mean?" he asked, moving slowly within me.

"My vagina isn't made of glass. You won't shatter it."

"It's your first time. Once you come, I'll move harder and faster."

"I'm only speaking from vibrator experience, but harder and faster will make me come harder and faster."

He paused, crooking his neck to peer down at me. "You don't say."

"I *do* say. Do it, Matis. You're going to make me scream."

He chuckled. "That's the point, love."

I adored it when he called me that. Did he mean it? I didn't want to think that he'd used the term with anyone else. It was mine. I wanted to own it, groom it, and cling to it for the rest of my days.

Shit. I didn't want to cling for the rest of my days. I sighed. Actually, I did.

"I'm going to scream at you if you don't let go," I said.

"You want that? It could hurt. It's your first time."

"Matis, you're not much bigger than my favorite vibrator."

"You keep mentioning this thing. What is it?" He kept moving slowly inside me. It was driving me closer to the edge, but it wasn't enough to push me over.

"It's a fake cock. I use it . . ."

"Ah." He grinned. "You enjoy fake cocks?"

"I want to enjoy the real one that's teasing me, but someone's holding it back."

"One dia, we will play with your fake cocks."

I had a feeling they'd never compare.

"Tell you what," he said, "I will show you what *my*

cock can do. You'll agree it's much better than a fake one."

With that, he started moving faster, varying his speed and how he hit my inner walls.

"Yes," I cried, running my palms over his chest, stroking his nipples. "This is almost as good as my Intergalactic Stud."

"What's a stud?" He pushed hard, picking up his pace. His spur hit my clit with each thrust, stroking across it.

It was all I could do to think. I was so close. Just a little more, and he was going to shoot me to the far reaches of the galaxy. "Stud is someone who services another. Sometimes for breeding, other times just to bring pleasure. That's the name of one of my vibrators."

"I'm better than your Intergalactic Stud."

"Prove it." I clung to his sides as my brain spiraled away. He really was better. My Intergalactic Stud had been upgraded, and there was no going back.

He reached down between us and pushed down on his spur, driving it against my clit.

My breath caught.

"Better, huh?" he asked with laughter spilling into his voice. "Scream for me, Tatum."

"Someone will hear."

"You think shrieking as you come will be frowned upon here?"

Good point.

His spur kept gliding across my clit, and when he pulled back, he dragged his fingers across it, twisting subtly, but with just enough pressure I couldn't hold back.

"Oh, yes. Yes." I released a guttural groan, and he moved faster, pistoning inside me with his thick, long cock. His spur kept hitting me just right.

Shuddering, I gave way, caught up in a storm that carried me to a distant shore.

He groaned above me, and his hot seed shot deep.

Then he wrapped his arms around me and tumbled onto the bed on his back, holding me to keep us connected.

I lay on his chest, realizing he'd ruined me for anything or anyone else.

CHAPTER EIGHTEEN
MATIS

Sex could do wonderful things for a person. Relax them. Make them feel like they're taller than a troolon. Give them enough energy to battle their strongest foe.

It could also create an unbreakable bond between two beings.

That was how I felt right now, connected to Tatum in a way that would last forever.

If I thought she'd take it, I'd hand her my heart. But I worried she'd throw it back at me.

I knew she'd enjoyed what we just did, but did she feel we'd shared more than the thrill of our bodies?

Loving someone was a force that overwhelmed the senses, a feeling that consumed the heart and soul. A fire that blazed true and would never burn out.

Did I love her? I was beginning to suspect I did.

I held Tatum while she dozed. When she woke, she

stroked my chest and shifted against me, nudging herself lower to embed my cock deeper inside her passage.

It didn't take more than that to spark the fire smoldering within me.

"Tatum," I said softly, her name like a bright light. No, a quasar.

"Don't talk," she said, rising over me. She started to move, lifting and falling back onto my cock, and there was nothing more beautiful than the sight of this woman taking her pleasure from my body.

I stroked her clit and nipples as she went higher. She moved faster, and our ragged breathing echoed in the room.

With a crash, she gave way, shuddering and quaking around me, her hoarse cry a balm to my soul. It was all my cock needed. Groaning, I shot everything I had deep inside her.

She collapsed on my chest, and I stroked her back, creating patterns with my fingertips.

"You need to feed me if you're going to keep that up," she said.

My laugh barked out. "You'll need to feed *me* if you're going to keep that up."

"Ha." She slid off me and climbed into the tub, gasping and shivering at the chilly temp. A quick wash, and she stepped out, loosely wrapping a cloth around her gorgeous body.

She brought the tray to the bed and juggled it while climbing onto my lap. We ate, and while the food was cold, it was the best meal I'd ever had.

After putting the tray in the hall, we climbed back into bed together.

I felt no shame in claiming her body once more. I'd never get enough.

We slept, rousing some time later. Darkness slanted through the room, broken only by a few street lights. It was unnatural night, of course. Since we all functioned better with regular cycles, the space station admins regulated lighting to simulate day and night, since a distant sun only generated intermittent muted light.

The tinny music that had echoed up from below had stopped, and I didn't hear even a muffled voice, something unusual for this place.

I slipped from the bed and crossed to the window, standing against the wall and peering around a slice of curtain.

Snuggles slunk from the bathroom where he'd slept. I scooped him up, stroking him while he purred.

A good-sized pack of Vessars moved below, slinking down the street. Their tails whipped back and forth, and each held multiple weapons. Nothing unusual about the weapons; they'd be foolish to move around on the space station unarmed.

They stopped across from this building and huddled together before separating, each group crossing the road and moving to surround us.

Fuck.

"Wake up, Tatum," I hissed. "We've got trouble." The credits I'd given Isirana had run out. She was still pissed off enough to squeal that I was here.

We dressed quickly, but when Tatum moved toward the door, I held her back.

"They've surrounded the building by now," I said softly. "We need to take a different way out."

Bangs rang out below, followed by a crash that I assumed was the front door slamming against the inner wall.

Footsteps stomped across the floor.

"Up you go," I told Snuggles, placing him on my shoulder. "Hold on." He dug in his claws and crouched, leaning against my neck while I lifted the window and peered out. "There's a small ledge below the window running around the building. And an alley below. The gap between this building and the next was too wide to jump."

"Go," she said, her wild gaze darting to the door. "They'll be here soon. We have to escape."

I stepped out onto the ledge, and Tatum joined me, gulping at the drop.

"Can you do it?" I hissed.

She jerked out a nod.

I moved carefully, continuing along the side of the building with Tatum close to my side. I was grateful the siding was uneven and we could find purchase.

Jumping to the ground didn't appear beyond my abilities, but the distance looked too far for a small human. I also wasn't confident about landing safely while holding her in my arms. If I twisted an ankle, I wouldn't be able to run. And I worried Snuggles wouldn't be able to hold on, and he'd fall.

Better to get farther away and find a place where we could make it to the ground safely—if such a place existed.

Following my lead, Tatum gripped the siding, moving along the ledge with me to the end.

The distance between this building and the steep roof of the one behind appeared closer than the one across the alley.

Shouts rang out, I assumed from our room, and a glance down revealed Vessars swarming the narrow gap between this building and the next. They weren't looking up. We had to act now.

"On my back," I said softly by Tatum's ear. "Grab my shoulders and hold tight."

She nodded, and I stooped down to make it easier for her, clinging to the wall while she climbed onto me.

"Ready," she said softly.

I leapt toward the other building.

CHAPTER NINETEEN
TATUM

I clung to Matis's shoulders as he leapt across a big gap between the brothel and the roof of the building behind it. My heart clambered up into my throat, and I closed my eyes and pressed my face into his back.

He landed lightly and kept going, scrambling up the roof to the top and down the other side.

"Again," he said, jumping to another building.

He kept going, leaping from one roof to another.

The shouts faded behind us, and a glance down didn't show anyone following on the streets.

Finally, he came to a stop, dropping to his knees. Snuggles jumped off his shoulder and raced to the edge of the roof to look down. He slunk back as I slid off Matis's back and leapt back onto Matis's shoulder again. He blinked at me, his tail snaking out to wrap around my wrist. I thought he'd claw me, but instead, he tugged me close and licked my hand.

Oh-kay. I wouldn't risk patting him right now, but maybe we weren't enemies any longer.

"What do we do next?" I asked softly.

"Can you give me your wrist com?"

My heart froze. "Why?"

"Mine was scrambled."

"Who'd do something like that?"

His gaze darted away. "I can't tell you."

Ah, so I wasn't the only one keeping secrets.

"Matis," I said in warning.

"Tatum," he said in the same tone. He held out his hand. "Your com."

It wasn't mine; the Ergeepelon gave it to me. It was all I could do not to put my arm behind my back. Without this com, I couldn't call for the alien to extract me.

But . . . Was I really going to follow through with my original plan? Things had changed. How could I betray Matis? I loved my mother. I'd do anything to save her life. But betraying someone else wasn't the way to do it.

I needed to tell him about my assignment, and I would, though now wasn't the time.

I slipped the device off my wrist and handed it to him.

He tapped into it and frowned before continuing. Glancing up, his gaze met mine. "We need to talk."

Shit. He knew. I hadn't told him; he'd found out on his own.

"I—"

He held up his hand. "Later."

My heart turned to stone. I wasn't innocent in this, but I hadn't done anything but sneak on board his ship. I clung to that fact. He'd believe me, right?

"Done," he said, a brief grin flashing on his face. He held up my com. "Firoh. You there?"

"Boss," Firoh said. "I was beginning to wonder what was going on with you and Tatum. Things look hot in a few areas on the space station. You need help?"

"Could you move us?" Matis asked.

Us.

My spine stopped quivering. For a secunda, I'd worried he'd leave me here. I could find my way off the roof, but without the statue or my com, there was no way I'd ever get home.

I didn't want to follow through on my original assignment any longer. I was falling in love with Matis, and the thought of leaving him was the same as ripping my heart from my chest.

"I've got a lock on you, Tatum, and Snuggles," Firoh said.

"Place us at these coordinates instead of pulling us in." Matis tapped on the screen.

"Really?" Laughter bubbled in Firoh's voice.

"Really."

"You're sure?"

"What's happening?" I asked.

Matis held up his hand between us. "On three, Firoh."

"Whatever you say, boss. Three . . . Two . . . and . . ."

Matis latched onto my hand. "Get ready."

"Where are we—?" My yip was cut off as a beam extracted us from the roof and dropped us . . .

A jolt, and I slammed into Matis. Snuggles hissed as we tumbled to the ground.

Bracing myself up on Matis's chest, I peered around, my sinuses assaulted by the muck surrounding us. "A dumpster, Matis?"

"Not a dumpster," he said, scooting out from beneath me. He rose and tugged me up to stand beside him. "We're inside the refuse processor."

Grinding sounds rang out ahead, and the ground shifted beneath us, jerking us toward the ear-piercing sound.

"Why?" I asked, breathing shallowly through my mouth. That wasn't any better; now I tasted the garbage in addition to smelling it.

"They won't look for us here."

"They won't need to find us once we've been turned into ground meat." I pointed to the end of the chute, the direction where the refuse—and we—were traveling toward at a fairly decent clip.

"I don't plan for us to get recycled," he said, peering up.

"If you've got another plan, then we need to act now." I gaped at the two-story munching jaws looming ahead. We'd be sucked in and scrambled, added to the rest of the station's refuse.

He leapt up, slamming his fist against a circular panel in the roof. A second hit made it give way, shifting to the side. A third hit caused it to bang as it flipped over and out of view.

"Are you ready for another ride?" he asked, his boots making squishing sounds on things I'd rather not examine. He tapped his shoulder and turned to present me his back.

Once he'd stooped down, I climbed on, holding tight. Poor Snuggles whimpered, glaring at a slimy mark on his side.

Matis jumped, grabbing onto the side of the hatch and levering himself—with me and Snuggles clinging—out through the hole. Once secure on the next level, he rose to his feet.

I slid off his back as he replaced the hatch over the compartment.

"You knew this was here," I said, looking around at where I found myself now.

"I assumed there would be access for repairs."

Robots zipped back and forth, ignoring us as they sorted through enormous containers of refuse. Metal and hard scrap would be compacted while compostable yuck would be dumped into the pit below. Once ground and pureed, enzymes would be added to speed up the breakdown process. Eventually, whatever was thrown away or unneeded would be turned into various items necessary to run the space station.

"This way," Matis said, nudging his head to the right.

I followed him along a metal platform shooting straight through the big room. "Why didn't you have Firoh remove us from the space station altogether?"

"I'm not finished here yet."

"You sold your cargo and the new one should be loaded by now."

He shot me a heavy glance. "Instead of quizzing me, why don't you explain why your com opened to an Ergeepelon communication hub?"

CHAPTER TWENTY
MATIS

I was stunned that her com took her to the Ergeepelon communication hub.

"About that," she said, her gaze darting to the droids humming along beside us, sorting refuse.

"Yes, about that."

"This isn't a good place to discuss it." She sucked in a breath and pushed it out. "I'm going to explain everything, but not here."

If her eyes hadn't filled with tears, I would've pressed her further.

Was she involved in whatever the Ergeepelons were doing? I was no closer to unveiling what they were covering up with the smuggling operation, and frustration poured through me. I didn't want to think she'd gotten mixed up in it, that she'd slunk onto my ship with a deceitful purpose.

It would make sense for them to infiltrate my ship if they suspected who I might be.

Why send a young human female, though? She'd stand out. Except she'd disguised herself as a boy.

She could be an agent herself, sent to seduce me into giving her information. A game older than the agency itself.

If she was a spy, she wasn't a very good one. An agent wouldn't have poked me in the side. They would've made sure they weren't in the hall where they could've been seen. They would've completed their mission and escaped the ship without me ever knowing they'd been there.

Unless she was a new, bumbling agent.

I hated to think this was true. It crushed me. But I wouldn't be the first agent to be seduced by a gorgeous female.

"I see what you're thinking," she said, taking my hand.

"I'm not sure you do." Even now, my heart reached out to her. Seeing tears in her eyes made me want to hold her, tell her everything would be alright.

I also wanted to shrug her off but, fool that I was, I tightened my fingers around hers as we reached the end of the room and a door. Beyond this, we'd have to take care. Firoh had placed us on the opposite side of the space station, but by now, the Vessars would've activated every pack.

They'd hunt us, and if we were lucky, they'd take us in for dubious questioning before eliminating us. At least then we'd stand a chance of escaping.

If we were unlucky, they'd shoot us without asking

questions. The fact that they hadn't tried to pop us off when I leapt from the roof suggested they wanted to quiz us first. Or quiz me, that is. I wasn't sure how Tatum played into this.

Cracking the door, I peered out, finding a long hall snaking to the right with doors on either side. Two droids hummed down the hall, away from us, but I had to assume they'd note our appearance and file a report with station admin. The Vessars would see the report within secunda and search our location.

I shut the door and leaned my back against it. "We wait for two droids to continue beyond our sight then rush out and find a place to hide."

"Things are not what you think," she said again.

"You're right. We can't risk speaking here." I needed time to harden my heart. If she cried or pleaded, I wasn't sure I could follow my training and do what needed to be done.

If she was involved in the smuggling operation, and she'd infiltrated my ship for a foul purpose, could I find the nerve I'd need to kill her?

CHAPTER TWENTY-ONE

TATUM

My heart ached. I could tell Matis suspected there was something fishy about me.

And he was right. I'd snuck onto his ship, stabbed him, then behaved as if I was nothing more than his cabin boy. To compound that, he might know my Ergeepelon boss. They could have bad history.

Once the droids had left the hall, we darted down the narrow passage. Snuggles bounced on Matis's shoulder from the motion and snarled, looking like he needed a nap. Me too. Stress had worn me out. And now I had a heartfelt conversation to look forward to.

At the end of the hall, we took a flight of stairs up one level and exited into yet another hall leading to a room marked Maintenance. Engines hummed behind the metal panel, but Matis didn't open the door. Spying a closet marked Janitor, he tugged open the door, moved buckets and mops to the side, and dragged me inside with him.

He put Snuggles on the floor, and the animal jumped into an empty bucket, where he dropped onto his haunches and blinked up at us.

Matis sat and hauled me down onto his lap, facing him with my legs around his waist. At least he wasn't pinning me to the wall with his claws.

"Talk," he said, tipping my chin up so I had no choice but to make eye contact.

"My mother has slyvarn. My dad gave it to her before he died in the war. Somehow, I've avoided catching it myself."

"Slyvarn alters your genetic make-up," he said grimly. "It's fatal."

"Mom's hung on for many yaros."

"I'm sorry. I know what it's like to lose family."

He'd lost everything in the war.

I hugged him, sad when he remained stiff in my arms. I understood why, though. He was protecting himself. I'd do the same.

"I've done my best to care for Mom," I said. "With the right medicine, she's able to mostly function."

He frowned. "They found a cure for it about a yaro ago. Why is she still sick?"

My chest hurt. He wasn't accusing me of neglecting her; I could tell he was surprised she hadn't been cured already. He didn't understand what it was like not to have everything you needed. I lifted my chin. "I can't afford the cure. I work hard. I make sure she always has food, a place to live, and medicine."

"I'm sorry. Why doesn't your government make the cure free?"

I shrugged. "I assume because they haven't finished lining their own pockets. Once they have more credits than they can spend in a thousand lifetimes, they might throw a few toward the little people, making them wealthy." My anger tasted bitter, and I didn't want to use that as a weapon against Matis, so I swallowed it down and sucked in a deep breath.

"You're here, not with her," he said. "How does your mother's illness tie into the Ergeepelon? Why did your com go to that hub?"

All or nothing, right? I couldn't hold this back from him any longer. I'd maintained a wall between us with my snarky demeanor, but inside, guilt churned through my guts.

"An Ergeepelon hired me," I said.

He went still. Only the tic on his left temple and the sharpening of his eyes gave away his tension.

"With the credits I'd make with this job, I could cure Mom. Not only that, but there would also be enough left over to keep us comfortable long enough for me to go to school and find a well-paying job. Our lives would be set."

"What job did the Ergeepelon ask you to perform?"

I sighed. "You know, Matis."

"Seduce me. Kill me?" His sharp tone hit me in the throat like a blade.

"No," I cried, trying to scramble off his lap. He held me in place. "I wasn't supposed to meet you at all."

"Yet you stabbed me."

His face was so grim. And anger sparked in his eyes.

"I didn't mean to stab you. It wasn't part of the job. It just . . . happened. You startled me. I scoped out your ship, and when I saw only droids, I assumed they ran everything. I didn't know you'd be on board."

His fingers tightened on my waist. "What did the Ergeepelon ask you to do?"

"I was supposed to sneak into the main stateroom and steal something." I nudged my head to my com that he now wore. He'd placed his own in his pocket. "Once I had it, I would engage the com, and they'd extract me. I'd be on my way back to Earth before I could blink."

"Steal," he said, his gaze focused inward. "Not kill me or sleep with me to . . . I don't know, gain information."

I tilted my head, watching his face. "What sort of information would they want me to lure out of you, especially using my not so delectable body?"

"It's delectable," he said sharply. "Never doubt that."

"I've never seduced anyone in my life," I said stiffly. "If I'm with someone, it's because I want to be, because I like them."

"If it helps any, I'm the same."

I'd like to think what we did meant something to him, but now I was worried. It felt like there was more going on here than just him being upset I was hired to steal something from his cabin.

"What did the Ergeepelon want you to steal?" he asked.

"An artifact." I frowned. "A statue? Well, from the

description he sent on the com, that's what it looked like. An alien lady looking up at the stars. It's supposedly in your safe, though I didn't see any evidence of a safe and believe me, I looked."

"If I had a safe, I'd keep it hidden so the prying eyes of a cabin boy wouldn't find it." The tic in his temple hadn't gone away. Neither had his hard expression and the grimness in his eyes. "A statue, huh?" He sucked in his lower lip. "It looks like we need to return to my ship."

"I don't expect you to forgive me. I've kept something from you. Lots of somethings, I guess. I understand if you're mad." My heart hurt more than it should have. He had every reason to be upset, but . . . Damn me for caring.

"You're an unwilling victim in all this," he said grimly. His fingers didn't relax on my waist.

He lifted his other arm. "And this is the Ergeepelon's com." He shifted me off his lap and stood. After wrenching the com off his wrist, he dropped it onto the floor.

He brought the heel of his boot down hard on it, and it shattered.

"Why did you do that?" My eyes stung with tears. I felt like he'd pressed a laser gun against my mom's head and pulled the trigger. "I can't get home to my mom without that. She only has enough medicine for half a lunar cycle. Matis . . ." I sagged against a cluster of cleaning tools, and they clattered together. "She's going to die."

"I'll make sure you get back to Earth before she runs out of medicine." He cupped my face in his big hands, turning my head this way and that, studying me as if he was seeing me for the first time.

I shouldn't care what he thought about me, but my heart stilled while I waited to hear what he'd say.

"Do you want the Ergeepelon tracking you?" he asked.

Shit. I should've thought of that. "It didn't occur to me. Why would he bother?"

"To make sure his asset didn't go rogue."

"Which I appear to be doing. That's the term, right, pirate captain? Going rogue?"

"Pirates epitomize going rogue."

"Somehow, you don't fit my image of a space pirate."

He stilled. "Why not?"

Snuggles looked from Matis to me, back and forth, as if he watched a sporting event between two rival players. He wasn't far off in that assessment, other than I sensed this match could mean life and death and not a cute prize for the winner.

"Because you're too honest." I held up my hand before he could speak. "I understand. You have honor. Enough integrity to instill trust. And I'm sure my ideas about space pirates are clichés, but you feel more like . . . I don't know. Someone who's more apt to obey the law than fly beneath its radar."

His lips thinned. "Maybe keep that impression to yourself."

"Who am I going to share it with, Snuggles?"

The beastie blinked at me, saying nothing.

"I've spilled my guts to you, Matis," I said. "Maybe

it's time you do the same?"

"I have nothing to spill," he said tightly.

"Then why aren't you meeting my eye?" My heart sunk to the refuse chamber a level below. "You don't *want* to share. I get it." I'd told him everything, endangering the job I was hired to do—which was shot now that the com was destroyed. Even worse, I'd endangered my mom.

And my heart.

But I would get through this, just like I did my dad's death, like I was preparing myself for my mom to die. I didn't need to give him the final piece of my soul.

"Don't do that," he said, gripping my shoulders.

"Do what?" I couldn't look up at him. Damn, if I did, I'd start to cry.

Why had I given him so much of me when it was clear he wasn't willing to meet me halfway?

"You're telling yourself what we have isn't special, and that's not true." He tilted my chin up, but I still couldn't meet his eye. "Look at me. Read me. Know you mean everything to me."

Pretty words without the kick to back them up. "I understand." My words came out dull, lifeless. "I was fun for a night, but you don't want entanglements. You're one of those honest pirates who's a loner. No need to clutter up your life with a woman like me."

His laugh snorted out. "Now, *that's* a cliché." He lifted me off my feet until our faces were level. "Look at me. Really."

All I saw was the guy I was falling for much too fast.

But no. I also saw a hint of vulnerability in his eyes.

"I'm in love with you, Tatum, for good or for bad," he said, his voice husky.

"You love me?" My eyes stung with tears.

He nodded.

"Why would that be bad?"

"Because I'm not at a point in my life where I have time for entanglements."

"Sometimes life hands you what you need at the right point in your life. It's up to you to take it or let it fall by the wayside. Maybe that's where you see me, Matis, despite feeling you love me. I'm convenient for you. I pretty much fell into your arms and your bed, and I've given you everything inside me that matters. But you've had fun, and it's time to toss me aside."

"Tatum." He pressed me against the wall and kissed me.

I wanted to resist him, but he made me go melty much too easily.

I tugged my face to the side. "Don't do this if you don't mean it. It's not fair."

"I love you, Tatum, and I want you in my life for the rest of my dias."

Frowning, I stared into his eyes, where I saw only my own reflection. "You just said you don't want entanglements."

"I said this wasn't the right time. But if I don't take this chance with you, I'll regret it for the rest of my life."

"Matis. What are you saying?"

"Be my mate, my love, my always. My forever."

CHAPTER TWENTY-TWO
MATIS

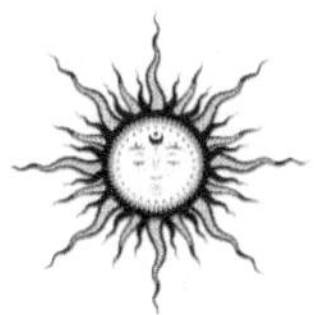

Who would've thought I'd propose a mating to someone while in the middle of an assignment that was obviously heating up? Especially someone I'd suspected could be a secret agent.

There was no denying the caring in her eyes when she looked at me and spoke of her parents. She was exactly who I thought she was when I met her; someone caught up in something without any idea of how dangerous it might be.

She wasn't part of my operation, yet she'd given me valuable information that might be the clue I've been looking for.

We needed to get to my ship and look at that statue.

As for my proposal . . . My sense of character might be completely off, but in my heart, I knew her. Tatum was an innocent caught up in a bigger plot that could get both of us killed.

"I don't know what you're asking me," Tatum said

stiffly. Her posture might still say she was ready to fight, but she wrapped her arms around my shoulders. Did she realize she was clinging to me as if I was her lifeline even when she was upset?

"I know we've barely scratched the surface of each other," I said. "We just met."

"We had sex."

I shook my head. "We made love. It wasn't just sex for me." Damn, were my emotions the only ones involved? No, that couldn't be true, not with so much hurt lingering in her eyes. "Maybe this isn't the right time to talk about our future. We're trying to avoid being killed."

"I think we have a few minue." Steel also lurked in her eyes. "Are you asking me to be with you?"

"On Earth, they call it marrying someone."

Tears sprung up in her eyes. "What a place to propose, Matis. Why aren't you on one knee?"

I started to put her down, determined to please her in any way possible.

"I was only teasing," she said, clinging tighter.

"I want to be with you, Tatum. I want to fly to Earth and make sure your mother is cured. I want to take her to the stars with us and show you both the wonders of the galaxies."

"I want to be with you," she said almost shyly. This tiny female who was my match both verbally and in bed was hesitant to show her feelings. I didn't want to roll right over her or press her, however.

"Take time to think about it," I said.

"I feel like you're holding something back from me, though I could be wrong. It's obvious I'm not a good judge of character, if my blithely taking the job with the Ergeepelon is anything to go by."

"I *have* been holding something back, and I'll explain once we're on the ship."

"Why not now? It appears we're relatively safe."

Because if I was caught or killed on our way to the ship, they'd be able to torture information from her. There were drugs they could use to make her tell them everything. The less she knew, the safer she'd be. Right now, she thought I was a space pirate, nothing else. If she was questioned, all she'd reveal was what she'd already told me. She'd taken a job to steal an object. She hadn't found the safe. She might reveal she'd made love with me, but she wouldn't be able to say much more than that.

They'd probably let her go.

If she knew everything, the odds were good they'd kill her.

"Alright," she said, her gaze locking onto mine. "I'm going to trust you in this. I *want* to trust you. And . . ." She sucked in a breath and pushed it out. "I may be incredibly stupid, but I love you too. I want to be with you." Her eyes pinched shut. "I can't believe I'm committing my future to a space pirate." She slid down my body to the ground. "You do know I'm not very good with weapons. And I don't want to get caught up in illegal activities. And I need to keep working somehow to pay for my mom's medicine. If we can, I want to go get her. She could remain with us while—"

"Tatum."

"What?" She frowned up at me.

"I promise you right now, we will not do anything illegal. We'll not only bring your mother medicine, but we'll also bring her a cure. And she can live with us."

"Her medicine is very expensive."

"I've been a very lucky pirate."

"No illegal crap, right?"

"Not unless you call smuggling food to those behind enemy lines illegal."

"I can live with that," she said. "No drugs, no illicit smuggling, no underhand crap if we're going to have a future together. Promise."

I held up my hand. "I swear."

"Then I'm yours, Matis, for as long as you want me."

"I want you forever. Got it?"

"Got it." She gave me a pert nod. "Then let's get our asses out of here before the lizard mafia find us."

"A wonderful idea, mate."

I engaged the mechanism to open the door.

It remained locked in place.

CHAPTER TWENTY-THREE

TATUM

"Is there a problem?" I asked Matis, studying the door latch that looked like any other I'd seen.

He jiggled it. "It's locked."

"This is a janitor's closet. It was unlocked when we entered. Why would it be locked now that we're inside?"

His lips thinned, and he started pulling on the knob.

"Oh. You think they know where we are and they're sending Vessars to retrieve us."

What if they'd tracked us through my com?

"Unfortunately, yes." When the door didn't budge, he looked around. His face cleared as he looked up. "Out we go." A jump, and he knocked aside a panel in the ceiling, revealing darkness. "Climb up me."

"And how will you get out?"

"Tatum." Warning came through in his voice.

Despite the tenuous situation, he needed to know one thing about me right now. I smacked my fists onto my hips. "If we're going to be partners—"

"So much more than that, sweetheart."

"Then we'll be equals."

He huffed. "You just said you needed guidance."

Really? "I just said I'm not the best with weapons. But I'm trainable, as you pointed out not long after you met me. And I've got this," I tapped my skull, "I want to be part of any decision that affects us both."

He pinched his eyes shut for a secunda. "Very well. If you'll climb my body, love, I'll boost you up through the ceiling and jump up myself."

"See? That wasn't hard, now was it?"

He grumbled as I climbed him like a tree. He really was ripped. I liked it. And I loved all the creative things he could do with his body.

When I was through the ceiling, I peered around. "Looks like an air duct." We'd be able to crawl through the small passage but not stand upright. Well, I might be able to shuffle along in a crouch, but not Matis.

He quickly joined me and replaced the panel, pointing to the channel behind me. "We'll go in that direction, putting our weight on the joints between the panels. If we're not careful, there's a good chance we'll fall through the panels."

"You knew this duct was here."

"I always study the schematic of any place I visit."

I huffed and turned, carefully making my way along the passage. "If I didn't know better, Matis, I'd think you were a spy and not a lowly pirate."

He chuckled, though he kept it low. "I'm anything but lowly."

He was right about that.

It wasn't easy moving from one support structure to another because of the wide panels between them. Matis found it easier with his bigger frame.

Wind whipped past us, and periodically, we'd hear voices and shouts below. We froze and moved on once whoever it was had moved past us. Vessars on the hunt, most likely.

Snuggles skipped ahead, his weight too slight to break through the panels. He periodically stopped and scowled back at us as if he wondered why this was taking us so long.

We didn't speak, not wanting to draw attention. We'd be easy pickings if they shot into the ceiling with lasers.

At least they couldn't track us, assuming he was correct in his belief that my com had been revealing our location. They'd seen I was with him when we left the ship.

We came to the end of the tunnel and a three-way intersection.

Voices echoed below us, but they lacked the urgency that would suggest they knew we were near.

I waved to either side, looking at Matis. Right or left?

He pointed to the hatch on the wall ahead, and we carefully made our way over to it. I moved to the side while he tried to open it.

Locked, I'd assume, and the touch pad to the right required thumbprint access. If he tested it, they'd be able to pin him down.

Frowning at the hatch, he grunted. He ran his fingers around the seam, ending at two hinges on the left side.

Pulling a blade, he slowly unscrewed the fasteners on the hinges, handing each one to me as he pulled it out.

The last one slipped from his fingers, plinking off the base of the tunnel.

My heart surged up into my throat, and my panicked gaze met his.

The voices below us stilled before rising to a boisterous chatter in a language I didn't understand.

Laser beams blasted up around us, searing through the panels and hitting the upper level that started to melt.

Snuggles yelped and scrambled up my shirt to perch on my shoulder. His tail whipped back and forth, and his claws dug into my flesh.

Matis ripped the hatch off the side wall and laid it on the floor. He lifted me and Snuggles, and tossed us through the opening, plunging through behind us.

"Go," I whispered, pointing to the metal channel running straight ahead of us.

Laser blasts continued to disintegrate the area outside the hatch, and from the sounds, the panels were crumbling, raining down on those trying to kill us.

This channel wasn't part of the duct system. From the schematic I'd studied earlier, and the roping wires tacked to the top of the passage, it was used solely to run power from one sector to another.

Snuggles leapt off Tatum and raced ahead of her.

Tatum scurried down the slope on her hands and knees, keeping low to avoid touching the wires. I assumed they'd be coated with some sort of protective substance, but it was a wise precaution to take. Live wires wouldn't be unheard of in a ragtag space station like this one. I followed her, and since we didn't need to worry about falling through the floor, we could move faster.

Snuggles shot terrified looks over his shoulder at us. Poor guy. I should've left him on the ship, though I doubted he would've allowed me to do so.

We left the laser blasts behind. I assumed Vessars were climbing up into the hole they'd made and would follow us. We had to move fast.

At the bottom, we came to a central electrical hub with thick bands of wires stabbing down the center of a two-story, round room, projecting into levels above and below. A door on the opposite side of the lower level stood open.

We scrambled to our feet, me tossing Snuggles onto my shoulder. I grabbed Tatum's hand and hurried her along a narrow platform encircling the room, slowly snaking down to the first level.

Racing through the door, we paused on the other side, taking in the hall stretching to our left and right.

I continued to the right with Tatum on my heels. We reached the end, and I wrenched open a door to a stairwell. This one wasn't part of the public area, so it was narrow. We couldn't take the stairs side-by-side.

"Two levels up," I said softly, nudging my chin in that direction.

We took the stairs fast and were both panting when we reached what was now the fourth level of the space station. Maintenance and infrastructure took up most of the three lower sections. The three highest levels had been purchased by those with incredible means. They lived above the masses, passing down rules and judgements. Regular people used the four levels in between for housing and commerce, and the remaining level contained multiple loading docks for ships putting into port.

"Our ship is docked on this level," I whispered as we rushed down a wide hall that slowly worked its way around the outer part of the space station in a circular pattern. We passed multiple air locks, and no one working inside the docking stations beyond seemed to pay us any attention.

Droids loaded with equipment and pulling hover trollies mounded with cargo eased to the side when we approached, but none sounded the alarm. They just hadn't been notified to look for us yet, though I wasn't sure why.

Shouts rang out behind us, giving me an idea. They thought they had us trapped already.

We broke into a run.

"Where's your ship?" Tatum asked, peering into each air lock we passed.

"Not far."

We ran harder while thuds rang out from behind us. The droids still ducked to the side, but I didn't have much hope they'd continue to do so. Soon, they'd be told to immobilize us.

When we reached the correct air lock, I engaged the door, and it swept open. We raced through and took the passage leading to my ship.

Firoh met us at the end, his eyes wide with worry. "Finally." He pivoted and hobbled toward the ship as fast as he could with his bum leg with us beside him. "Ship's loaded. I made sure they didn't plant bombs or trackers. I've got clearance to depart, but we need to be out of here before they pull it and engage the locking mechanisms."

If the station did that, even full thrusters wouldn't be able to break the hold they'd place on our ship. They'd have us pinned and could do whatever they pleased with us. Even locking our outer hatch wouldn't make a difference. They'd use borers to gain access through the underbelly of the hull.

We scrambled up the ramp.

"Cutting it close, boss," Firoh said, his gaze and weapons trained at the area we'd come from. He backed inside behind us and closed the hatch before racing down the hall as fast as he could go. "Find a secure place to settle and fast. I'll be on the bridge."

"My cabin," I told Tatum, hurrying her in that direction.

When we were inside, I tossed Snuggles into his secured crate. He snarled and swiped out at me, but I'd only keep him inside until we were clear. Once his door was latched, I tugged Tatum over to my chair. Sitting, I strapped us in.

The ship hummed and shifted.

A grating sound rang out, and Tatum's wide eyes met mine.

"Outer space station hatch opening," I said. "I hope." If not, they'd already engaged the borers.

I opened a drawer in my desk and pulled out my spare wrist com, putting it on.

"Report," I barked into it.

"Lifting off now, captain," Firoh said, tension thriving in his voice.

"Anything from station admin?"

"Not so far. We—"

Alarms sounded on the bridge, and a computer voice erupted overhead.

"Stand down," the computer said. "Prepare to be boarded."

"Fuck that," Firoh said.

The ship shuddered and subtly swayed.

"Hold on," Firoh shouted. "Come on, baby. Don't fail me now."

Facing me, Tatum clung to my shoulders. "Will we get away?"

"Firoh will make it happen." A hot-shot pilot, he'd flown more missions in the military than he could count. He was decorated and could've retired ages ago on the financial rewards his government had bestowed upon him. But he loved flying and even more, he loved working for the Interstellar Interpol. I'm really going to miss him once he gets word about his sons and leaves.

If my mission wasn't completed, and the odds of that didn't look good, the agency would send someone else to replace him. I could pilot the ship, but I had enough to deal with already. That, and it looked better if I had at least one crew member completing tasks, rather than me handling everything. Few pirates did it all themselves.

The ship shuddered, and a grating whine rang out. Tatum clung to my arms, her eyes wide and her breathing rapid.

"Are we clear?" I asked through my com.

"Kind of busy right now," Firoh shouted. "The space station doesn't seem happy we're departing so soon."

"Have we undocked?"

"Affirmative. We've made it through the hatch, but they're trying to pull us back." He swore, and the ship listed to one side. The few items not strapped down tumbled across the room, creating loud bangs.

Snuggles hissed, making me grateful I'd secured him in his crate. Most everything was tied down; otherwise, someone could be hurt by flying objects, including him.

"Why are they so determined to keep us from leaving?" Firoh asked. "What did you do?"

My lips twisted. "Who says I did anything?"

"Wouldn't be the first time," he grumbled.

"I met with a friend. He died before we could finish our conversation."

Silence reigned for a minue.

"Vessar," I added.

"Fuck," Firoh snarled. "I'm sorry."

"Yeah." The guy hadn't been a true friend, just a contact set up by another agent, but someone somewhere would mourn his loss.

More screeches rang out, followed by the ship's engines roaring. A snap, and we suddenly went weightless.

"Broke free of the hold," Firoh shouted. "Yay, baby. Come on! Engaging thrusters. Hold on to your asses down there, Captain."

A pop, and everything went silent.

"What happened?" Tatum asked, her voice shaking.

"They tried to hold us back, but Firoh and my ship weren't having it."

"This ship is a hunk of junk," she said.

"It only looks that way. It's wearing a disguise."

She snorted. "You're telling me it's not actually falling apart?"

"Not at all." I needed to share as much with her as I could. Some information had to be held back. Agency protocol and all that. But I could tell her enough so she'd know what was going on.

"We've put enough distance between us and the space station," Firoh said. "You can relax now."

"Thanks, friend," I said, ending the communication. I released our restraints, and Tatum climbed off my lap.

"Snuggles wants to come out?" she cooed, moving to the crate. After my nod, she opened the front. Snuggles leapt out and scrambled up her clothing until he could perch on her shoulder.

She struck a jaunty pose. "Guess I've got a pirate companion now."

Snuggles rubbed his head against hers and started to purr.

"We can share him," I said, glad my fuzzy friend had accepted my mate. But was she my mate? She hadn't said yes. In the turmoil of trying to escape the space station, I hadn't pressed her.

She'd mostly committed, however. She'd told me she loved me.

We'd figure out our future once we'd solved the riddle of the statue.

"Where to next, boss?" Firoh asked through my com.

I gave him coordinates.

"Once that's set, I'm going to the galley," he said. "Anyone hungry?"

Tatum nodded.

"Plan to feed us both," I said.

"Will do, boss," Firoh said. "Give me a few minue."

"While we wait," I told Tatum. "I believe it's time I told you who I really am."

CHAPTER TWENTY-FIVE

TATUM

I didn't like that I knew so little of what was going on. Matis had secrets, but I was grateful he was prepared to share them.

"You're not a pirate, are you?" I said as the thought occurred to me. "Firoh isn't one either." I wasn't sure how I knew this, but the certainty of it felt right.

"What gave us away?"

I shrugged. "I'm not sure it was one single thing. Just a hunch."

"We're interstellar agents."

"Ah." That made sense, but the thought of it shuddered through me. I slumped on the bed and placed Snuggles beside me. He curled into my thigh and blinked up at me, looking as stunned as me, though his concern must come from being crated and the danger tainting the air. I stroked his fur, and he settled, purring.

"Ah?" Matis said. He stooped down to the floor in

front of me and took my hand, squeezing it. "What does that mean?"

"Just that. Ah. I knew something was off, but I couldn't pin down what it might be. I didn't suspect this, though. I thought . . . I guess I thought maybe you'd stumbled into this. That maybe you lived in a colony in the outer galaxy, that your community needed supplies, food, maybe? That you patched up this ship and were doing what you could to keep everyone from starving."

"Funny how you named my dream job."

"Stumbling around pirating?"

Grinning, he shook his head. "Living in a colony, doing supply runs to provide things we can't grow or produce ourselves." He continued to stare up at me earnestly. "I do make sure outer galaxy colonies have first dibs on my cargo, and I often transport food and needed supplies at a very low cost, but that's all part of my cover."

"I'm surprised you can tell me this."

He settled on the bed behind me and tugged me into his arms with me facing him. "I trust you."

I snorted. "I'm surprised. I snuck on your ship intent on stealing, stabbed you, and then pretended to be a boy."

"It was our first date."

I couldn't hold back my grin. "Maybe it was."

"You had a good reason, and it was only a little poke."

We started kissing, and it wasn't hard to get caught up in the minue, in him. Yeah, we had other things to talk about, but I wanted to be with him again. My skin craved his touch, and my heart needed this connection.

Snuggles huffed and leapt off the bed, disappearing into the bathroom.

I slid my fingers beneath his shirt, needing to feel his skin.

"Matis," I moaned. I helped him out of his shirt and started kissing his neck, moving to his chest and downward. He shucked his pants with my help, and his cock bobbed up, eager. I wanted to feel it inside me, but I needed to taste it first.

"Oh, yeah . . ." he groaned when I licked the tip. It looked so good, so perfect with its thick head. His bronze skin was lighter here, and the nubs along the side of his cock felt soft yet firm beneath my tongue.

I licked up and down the shaft, gliding my lips across the head with each pass. I took as much of him as I could into my mouth and sucked, tasting him for the first time, letting my mouth get used to the feel.

His hoarse cry rang out, and he thrust into my mouth. I took him deeper, wishing I could take all of him. I started sucking him, bobbing up and down on his cock, savoring the feel of those numbs gliding back and forth across my lips. They'd pleasured me earlier, and I couldn't wait to feel them inside me again.

"Tatum . . . Yes . . ."

I slid my mouth off him and nibbled down his shaft. Sucking his balls into my mouth, I ran my tongue across them. I wanted him to be ready. I wanted him hard and wild when he pushed inside me.

He started to rise, to urge me beneath him, but I put my hand on his stomach and pressed him back onto the pillows.

I was greedy. I needed more.

"Let me take care of you, Matis," I whispered, holding his gaze as I lowered my lips to the side of his shaft. He stroked my hair, weaving his fingers into it, holding tight, clinging to me like I did to him when he did something similar to me.

I kissed my way up and down, then took him into my mouth again. I slid my lips down as far as I could go and sucked, trying to take all of him. He bucked beneath me, a writhing mass of pleasure, his groans echoing in the room. His cock tightened. His balls shifted.

I pulled back, letting his cock go with a pop.

He gazed into my eyes as I stripped quickly. I climbed on top of him and spread my body wide. He hadn't even touched me other than a few kisses, and I was already dripping, more than ready to feel him pumping inside me.

I angled his cock so that he'd hit my sweet spot on the first thrust.

With our gazes locked, I sank onto him, pushing down, stretching, gulping as he filled me. Finally, my butt rested against his thighs. Deep within me, he throbbed, and his perfect spur hit me just where I needed attention.

His hands wrapped around my hips. "Ride me, Tatum," he growled. "I need to feel you come. Shudder around me, mate. Take everything you need and then do it again."

"This—you—mean everything to me," I said, rising and sinking back down. My eyes were rolling back in their sockets. There couldn't be anything better than the feel of him buried deep inside me. Those nubs along his length stroked me, a few gliding across my G-spot.

He lifted me, then pushed me back down hard, slamming his cock deep within me with a jerk of his hips. His breathing raged, and his need lit my veins on fire. Flames licked through me like a fuse heading toward a mound of explosives.

Leaning forward, I rode him while he pushed up to meet each of my thrusts. My heart slammed against my ribs, and my pulse thundered in my ears. All I could focus on was the feel of his cock pushing and pulling, stroking within me.

He was so much bigger than me, but he somehow curled himself up so he could wrap his arms around me. Our lips met. He kissed me hard and deep, pushing his tongue into my mouth while his cock did the same with my body. I sucked on his tongue before his mouth moved to my neck.

My orgasm was building, a rocket about to blast into the outer galaxy. He was going to push me over the edge, and there would be no holding back.

He moved his hands from around me so that his claws glided across my nipples. Leaning forward, he sucked on the tender skin of my neck.

When he pinched and rolled my nipples between his fingers and a scream of pleasure escaped my lips.

I came, my body jerking, my head thrust back. My moan shot toward the ceiling as my body succumbed again and again. I kept moving, pushing down hard on his cock even as the last fingers of pleasure zinged through me.

Matis pulled out of me and rose above me, turning me so I knelt in front of him on my hands and knees.

He thrust his cock into me, and I groaned at how amazing it felt. My inner walls still quivered, and I didn't think I could handle any more.

Then he started moving, holding my hips in place while thrusting full and deep within me. Each lunge pushed me up farther, and my passage clenched around his cock, milking him.

He started pumping faster, and one of his hands slid beneath me. He ran a claw across my engorged clit.

I buried my moans in his pillow as I started spiraling into the sky all over again.

Damn, I was ruined for anyone but him. No one and nothing were ever going to compare.

I wanted him to feel this way too, this amazing sensation of completeness. Rightness. My heart throbbed, overcome with emotions. I wanted him to know this connection and bond between us was real, that it meant everything to me.

"Matis, I love you."

"Tatum," he hissed. "I . . ."

"Yes," I cried, thrusting back to meet his cock. My body started clenching. I couldn't hold on for long.

He stroked my clit and curled over me, nibbling on my shoulder before licking. "Mate. My precious mate."

My core exploded, and I came, milking him deeper. I felt his cock pulsate, felt his warmth fill me as his body shook above mine. I cried out, my voice hoarse from emotion. I'd never been so happy in my life, feeling him come with me, his body encircling, sheltering mine. I'd never felt so complete, so perfect.

He eased backward, rolling with me lying on top of him. I was able to shift around with him still locked inside me. I needed to see him, to gaze into his eyes. He gave me a soft, almost vulnerable smile as his hands roamed my back and butt. "You're so beautiful, Tatum," he sighed. "Just . . . wow."

"Wow? You're the amazing one, you know that, right?" I ran my fingers through his hair and kissed his chest. Locked together, I couldn't quite reach his mouth.

"I love you," he whispered.

I lay in his arms while my heartrate returned to normal. Would it always be like this between us? I had a feeling it would be. We were made for each other both physically and emotionally. He was easy to love. I wanted to cherish him, hold him, and make sure no one ever hurt him.

I must've dozed, because I woke suddenly when he started to shift me onto the bed.

"Come back here," I said as he stepped onto the floor.

He leaned over me, his mouth slanting across mine, and that was all it took to heat me up once more.

Lifting away, he grinned. "You are incredibly tempting, mate, but we have work to do."

I sat up. "What's on the agenda, boss?"

"Would you like to take a look at that statue?"

CHAPTER TWENTY-SIX
MATIS

"Ah, so that's where you hid your safe," she said as I unlatched and opened a mechanical porthole near the head of my bed, revealing the hidden compartment. "Cool." She strolled closer, studying the porthole. "You used a computerized mirror image of what we'd see outside. No one would ever think a safe was hidden behind it. Who'd want to open a porthole in space? They'd be sucked through the opening and die within secunda."

"Exactly." Pressing my thumbprint against the panel on the front of the safe itself resulted in a click. I swung the door open.

"The safe was built into the outer wall."

"I had it specially designed. I told you my ship is not the hunk of junk it appears to be."

"It's amazing." Her sparkling eyes met mine. "Not necessarily your ship. I'm still undecided about that, but the safe."

"It's not very large but I find it useful."

Tatum crowded closer, frowning as she peered into the small opening. "Interesting stuff in here, Matis."

I nudged aside a pile of small devices. "These are programmed with schematics of more planets and installations than I'll ever have time to review."

"You never know when you might need to sneak onto an enemy planet."

"I try to avoid sneaking anywhere, hence the pirate ship cover."

"If it helps any, you had me fooled. The eye patch that I notice you only wear when you're outside your cabin made me suspicious. Your clothing doesn't necessarily fit a pirate's swashbuckling ways."

Grinning, I tugged her into my arms, lifting her so I could kiss her. "You enjoy my swashbuckling ways."

She cupped my shoulders and nuzzled my neck. "You can swashbuckle your way all over me whenever you please."

Which I wanted to do all dia long. Unfortunately, duty called, and if I wasn't on my toes at all times, I'd get caught—and wind up an agency statistic.

I lowered her to the floor. She grabbed one of my shirts and tugged it on, sadly covering up her naked body. My shirt was comically large on her, hanging to her knees, but I liked seeing her wearing my things, covering herself up in me.

She rolled up the sleeves and joined me at the safe again.

I'd piled small, worn bags of credits behind the

devices, and I tugged them out, tossing them onto my bed to get to the things I'd placed behind.

Tatum lifted one of the bags, weighing it in her hand.

"Ready made for bribes," she said, whistling softly.

"Check this out." I carefully opened a small wooden box and pulled out the soft bag inside. Once I'd untied the top, I slid a clear crystal out onto my palm. It's strange, soothing melody drifted through the room.

Tatum gasped. "What is that?"

"A Vikallian soothing crystal. The Vikallians mine them on the meteors orbiting one of their moons. They're quite rare."

"Is it alive?"

"Not as far as anyone knows. It grows in an oxygen-free environment until it's mined. I suppose crystals like this might be able to grow anywhere. No one knows."

Her finger hovered above it until I lifted it closer, urging her to touch. When her fingertip glided across the smooth, glossy surface, its voice grew louder. "It's beautiful," she said in awe, as mesmerized as I was when I first saw it.

"A Vikallian gave it to me."

"Spoils of your pirating trade?"

"A gift. I rescued his younglings after they were kidnapped." Nearly losing my life in the process, but I'd risk my life again to do it any dia of the week. Younglings should never be used for blackmail or trafficked in any way.

"Admirable."

"All in a dia's work."

She looked up at me. "I imagine there's quite a story there. I'd love to hear it someday."

I nodded. "I'll share it." I had a feeling I'd be sharing everything with Tatum from now on.

Which brought up our future—mine in particular. If she was a fellow agent, one of us would have to leave the agency. Fraternization wasn't forbidden, but if a relationship became permanent, one of the pair could not remain within the organization. They worried one of us might try to manipulate the other. And they knew an agent would sacrifice anything to ensure their loved one was safe, even if that meant betraying the organization.

A partner not in the agency could be used in the same way, but they were given protection to keep them safe while one agent was on assignment.

"Can I hold it?" Tatum asked, shooting me a longing look.

"Of course." I dropped it into her open palm.

My gasp echoed hers.

For the first time, the crystal shifted, the sharper edges of its triangular shape smoothing until it formed an oval. Its musical tune changed, another first, releasing a bright melody.

"Whoa," she said.

"I've never seen that happen."

"It's so cool." She gazed at it in wonder.

"The Vikallian said the crystals sometimes bond with a person." I nudged my chin toward it. "I'd say that's happened. It's yours now."

"Oh, no, I can't take it." She tried to give it back, and the humming rose in volume, becoming more shrill.

"It belongs to you. Or you to it, I suppose. I don't know much more about crystal bonding than that, but I can message my friend and see if he'll share more information."

"Why would it bond with someone?"

I shrugged. "I've only heard rumors stating the crystal can give aid in its bond mate's time of need."

"Huh."

I gave her the soft pouch. "Keep it with you as much as possible. I don't know if the rumors are true, but what if they are?" I supported anything that might keep her safe.

She slid it into the pouch reverently and it stopped singing. Tucking it into her pants, she puffed out a breath. "It's . . . I don't know what to say. I've never heard of anything like this. I'm honored." She blinked slowly, her head tilting as if she heard something I didn't. "Wow."

"What?"

"When I said I was honored, the crystal warmed in my pocket."

I definitely needed to reach out to my Vikallian friend soon for more information about the crystal.

Turning back to the safe, I removed a few encoded plates containing self-destruct systems I hoped I never had to use.

"A contact sent this to me about six lunar cycles ago," I said, finally pulling out the wrapped statue. "He said to protect it with my life, and he lost his own life getting it to me."

Too many friends and colleagues had died to preserve the safety of all living beings within the galaxies. Again, I wondered if I wanted to remain in this career or cede it over to those who were younger and more willing to sacrifice everything. I still burned to protect as many beings as I could, even if that meant losing my life, but with a mate and perhaps, someday, a youngling or two, I felt a sense of responsibility to one person above all others, something I hadn't experienced before.

Just as I'd be devastated to lose Tatum, she felt the same—of this I was certain.

I couldn't endanger myself by remaining in this job; it wasn't fair to someone I loved.

What would I do if I didn't continue with the agency? Perhaps it was time to find out. I wouldn't quit until I'd seen this current job through, but after that . . .

Tatum and I would need to talk about this. Despite mentioning my dream of doing supply runs to under-served colonies, I couldn't make a decision like this alone.

When I sat on the bed, Tatum joined me, leaning into my side, watching as I unwrapped the statue on my lap.

"Interesting," she said, peering at it.

About the length of my forearm, the minteen wood it had been carved from gleamed in the low light. I held it upright.

"It's Ergeepelon," I said.

She tapped one of the six limbs, each ending in a lethal spike. "Looks like my former boss."

"You have no boss now," I said. "You're your own person."

"I quit, I guess, since I'm not willing to do what he asked. And I guess I quit your cabin boy position, too, though I'll be happy to scrub your back if you return the favor."

Her smile made my skin hum.

"Deal," I said. "I don't know why my contact made sure I received this, but his missive told me to protect it with my life and make sure the Ergeepelon rulers never learned I had it. To destroy it if anyone suspected it was in my possession." There had to be a reason for this, but nothing about the figurine revealed a clue. "We have to figure out why it's so valuable to them or follow through with their suggestion and destroy it. Many died to make sure it was well-hidden."

She took it from me. "Heavy." Turning it, she examined it from all angles.

"Honestly, I haven't looked at it since I received it. I stuffed it in the back of my safe and mostly forgot it existed."

"The Ergeepelon knows you have it." She frowned, staring at the back of the statue where the Ergeepelon's spikes jutted from the creature's spine. When she glided her finger across them, the crystal in her pocket released one high-pitched note before going silent.

"Let me have it," I said, holding out my hand. If the

crystal sensed it could harm her, it would sound an alert. Was that what was happening?

A soft click rang out from the statue.

Tatum dropped it on the bed as if it had suddenly become hot.

The back of the statue fell off, revealing a hidden compartment.

CHAPTER TWENTY-SEVEN

TATUM

"Did I break it?" I asked, though I doubted that was the case. The back panel had come off easily, and it had smooth sides like the statue had been built that way.

"I don't think so." He shot me a surprised look. "I'd say you've revealed the statue's secret and perhaps why the Ergeepelon are willing to kill to find it." He swallowed and stared at the statue, not touching it. Pulling a knife, he dragged the back panel away from the base, revealing more of the insides.

With the tip of his knife, he carefully extracted a long, thin object wrapped in an oiled cloth.

"What do we have here?" he asked.

Curiosity battled with terror inside me. The Ergeepelons were willing to kill to obtain this. What could it be?

"Do we dare touch it?" I asked.

"It could be dangerous." He grabbed a second blade and used the two tips to slowly unwrap the object.

"Is it metal?" I asked as we stared at a tube the thickness of my finger and about twice the length. A series of gears jutted out from the surface in a circular pattern, winding around the object.

He tapped it with his knife, and it clinked. "Perhaps."

The crystal released a discordant hum in my pocket, a warning I'd be wise to heed. I'd found a friend who was determined to protect me, and I wasn't sure what I thought about that. I'd been drawn to the crystal from the moment I saw it, as if it had absorbed a bit of me when I touched it. When it shifted in my palm, I got the impression it gave me something of value. I just didn't know what that could be yet. Hopefully, I'd never have to find out.

"It looks like a fabricated part," I said.

"I think I know what it is." His grim gaze met mine. "Agency intel suggests the Ergeepelon have found a long-abandoned disintegrator ray."

"I'm not sure what that is, though the name makes it sound deadly."

"Rumors say they unearthed the ancient device on the planet Zoron. The Zorons are long since extinct, but their tech was much more advanced than anything in the galaxies today. It's said they warred with another species and used the ray in the final battle. The ray destroys organic material, and those delivering the death sentence to their enemies killed themselves."

"People, animals, anything living." My belly churned; I worried I was going to get sick. "If the Ergeepelons have a weapon like that, it would completely change the interstellar landscape. They could threaten to use it to get whatever they wanted and it would be delivered." She frowned. "But what would keep them from dying themselves? The Zorons left a good lesson behind."

"If I found the ray and planned to use it, I'd make sure I could protect myself and those around me. While I'm sure they'd love to blackmail everyone in the galaxies, I suspect they have a more local target in mind, at least for their first challenge."

I sucked in a breath. "They've been warring with the Talaxians for a long time."

"They want a mineral-rich moon they insist the Talaxians stole from them."

"Didn't the interstellar court rule that they had no right to possession?"

"Yes," he said. "But they continue to grumble."

"If they annihilate every Talaxian, they can take the moon for themselves."

"Exactly."

"Who'd challenge them after that? They'd risk the Ergeepelons pointing the ray in that direction." I slumped on the bed, horror scorching my bones. "How are the Vessars involved in this?"

"I'm not sure they are, though it wouldn't surprise me. They're the Ergeepelon's strongest allies. They'd love to gain access to Talaxian mines and broad plains containing rich soil."

"I wonder if they've come to an agreement. The Vessars take the plains and mines, and the Ergeepelons take the moon."

"If the ray exists, that would be my suspicion."

"And you think they have the ray?"

"The intel we received suggested an Ergeepelon had located it, though there were missing components. But when our contacts looked into it, they didn't find much evidence."

I poked the statue. "This is evidence, don't you think?"

"It's certainly suspicious." He frowned at the metal component. "The few who were underground survived the Zoron final battle. Horrified by what their rulers had done, they broke the device and scattered the components throughout the galaxy."

"Why didn't they incinerate it?"

"It's made of a material unlike anything else in the galaxies. It can't be burned or melted."

"It must've been melted to form the pieces," I said.

"They added material that changed its chemical compound. The Zorons really were smart."

"Until they killed themselves," I said dryly.

He nodded. "Rumor has it the Ergeepelons have found most of the parts and have assembled them, though they're missing a few." He tapped the metal object with the blade of his knife. "I'll run some tests on this, but I suspect it could be part of the ray."

Suddenly chilled, I tugged a blanket up over my body. "We need to stop them."

"I need to reach out to my handlers. This is bigger than anything I want to tackle with just Firoh's help."

"What was your full assignment?"

"I've been investigating a Vessar-Ergeepelon smuggling operation, trying to discover what it might be hiding. The statue made its way to me through my contacts, but I assumed it was just one of the items stolen from a planet where its civilization had died out."

"And now we suspect it's much more than that."

"I assume they steal artifacts and sell them to fund their ongoing search for the missing disintegration ray components. And they're searching while they're stealing treasure. If all this is true, I bet they found components in the cities on lost worlds."

"If we tell your handlers, they'll put more agents on the case, right? This is huge. If they finish reconstructing that ray, they'll rule the galaxies. All they'll need to do is point the ray in a planet's direction and make demands." This would change the world order. No one would be safe.

"We need to act fast." Lifting the metal object, he held it up in the light. "Our intel suggested they might be missing only a few components. This could be the last."

CHAPTER TWENTY-EIGHT
MATIS

After sending Tatum to the galley to get us something to eat, I grabbed one of the spare wrist coms from my safe, sat at my desk, and ran some tests on the object. Zoron metal had distinctive qualities not found anywhere else in the galaxies, and the ray gun was rumored to contain bits of cordiavium, the component that made it nearly indestructible despite the alterations they made so they could destroy it.

Before I contacted my handlers, I had to make sure this truly could be part of the ray and not some random piece of metal hidden inside a statue for an unknown reason.

After analyzing the object, my com beeped, and I read the readout on the screen.

"Conclusive," I hissed. "It contains cordiavium. It must be part of the disintegrator ray." I'd truly wanted to be wrong. Now we had to act fast.

I placed a call to the agency.

I waited patiently while the connection was made, my signal bouncing from one satellite to another. When it didn't connect in a timely manner, I frowned at the com. Hanging up, I ran the call again, tapping my fingers on the metal device.

Again, I couldn't connect.

"Firoh," I said into the com.

"Yeah, boss?"

"My com call won't go through to headquarters."

"Let me look into it."

"Thanks." Ending our communication, I picked up the metal object again, studying it from all angles. A small symbol on the bottom caught my eye. Zoron, which was further confirmation of its origin.

"Hey, boss?" Firoh said. "A debris field has damaged the Krell Satellite. They hope to have it repaired in a few dias or so."

"Why so long?"

"They have to transport parts to the satellite. Sorry, but signals won't go through at all until it's back in commission."

I frowned. "Thanks."

That's when I remembered the disc the Vessar gave me back at the bar before he was murdered. In the hubbub, I'd forgotten all about it, a foolish move on my part.

I pulled it from my pants pocket and flipped it over, wondering what it could be. It was made of a simple silver metal and about half the size of my palm and a pinch thick. I tried to pry it apart at the seam with the tip of my knife, but it remained locked up tight.

Tatum bustled into the room with a tray of food, and I laid it on my desk to examine later.

Her smile made me grin. I still couldn't believe I'd found my mate, the only person who could make me complete. And she wanted to be with me.

She placed the tray on the desk and strolled around it, climbing into my lap, facing me. We kissed, and I wanted to sweep the tray off my desk, lay her back on the smooth surface, and claim her all over again. But Firoh would have a few choice words for me if I wasted the food he'd put effort into preparing.

She leaned back in my embrace and traced her fingers across my chest. "I still can't believe we're together."

"I love you, Tatum."

Leaning into me, she sighed. "Matis. I'm in love with you too."

Forget the food.

I lifted her and carried her to my bed.

"What's this?" she asked.

We'd eventually made it to the meal, though it was cold. She sat on my lap, feeding me while I fed her, a silly thing that made me incredibly happy.

She lifted the disc, turning it over.

"My Vessar contact gave it to me before he died," I said.

"It must have meaning then." Her solemn gaze met mine. "Do you think it's another part of the disintegrator ray?"

"It's not Zoron metal." I'd tested it.

"It looks like it could open." She traced her finger along the seam encircling the disc.

"I tried to pry it open." I grabbed my knife, determined to get inside it this time.

Squinting, she ran her fingernail across the seam. "There's a little button here and—"

The disc split open and projected a hologram image above it.

"Whoa," she said, holding the disc up in her palm.

A space island spun in front of us.

"What do you think it is?" she asked.

"A space island."

"Why die to get that image to you?" Her eyes widened. "Do you think it involves the ray?" Her breath caught.

"Perhaps."

"What *is* a space island?"

"Space islands are a strange phenomenon," I said. "They defy every scientific theory out there. Unlike a planet, they consist of large strips of land often surrounded by water or boiling pits of toxic substances. Each has their own gravity, often similar to Earth."

"I've never heard of them," she said in awe.

As we watched, the holoimage zoomed in closer,

displaying a small, ragtag town of low-level buildings and a somewhat more advanced spaceport some distance away. One road led from the spaceport to the town. As we watched, the holoimage focused on a decrepit warehouse on the edge of town.

It winked out after that.

"Interesting," Tatum said.

"I assume he wants us to focus our investigation on that warehouse."

"Us?" I asked, my heart stilling.

"You don't think I'm going to let you continue this on your own, do you? We're in this together." A hint of vulnerability came through in her voice, but not to manipulate me or make me declare myself, which I'd already done.

"You're not an agent."

"I'm not," she agreed. "But we're a team."

"Actually . . ."

"What?" she asked.

"I proposed, but I don't believe you gave me an answer."

She barreled into me. "Yes, yes, yes." Leaning back in my embrace, she smiled. "Back to our discussion."

I chuckled, admiring her determination, but I wasn't going to relent. "I don't want to risk you."

"Yet you'll risk yourself," she asked. "How do you think that makes me feel?"

"I'm a trained agent; you're not."

"We could argue all dia," she said with a sigh.

"I won't argue about this." My tone made it clear my

decision was final. Sharing information with her was enough. When I took on this challenge, I had to know she was secure wherever I left her.

She frowned but didn't say anything further about going to the island. I suspected she wasn't done with the topic, however.

"Do you recognize the island?" she asked.

"It's Nebula's Nest."

She frowned. "Never heard of it." A frown filled her face. "How far is it from Talaxian?"

How had I thought I could keep her out of this? For a non-agent, she was savvy. "It's located between Talaxian and Ergeepelon, well within shooting distance of Talaxian."

She blinked. "It might be a coincidence, but do you think...?"

I finished the thought for her. "I suspect they're reconstructing the disintegrator ray there. If they're able to make it functional, they'll use it to eliminate the Talaxians from the safety of the island. Then they won't endanger their own people on their home planet."

"We have to destroy the ray; it's the only way we can give the Talaxians a fighting chance. And if we can gather enough evidence before we destroy the ray, we can share that with the interstellar federation. They'll punish the Ergeepelons, and I assume intervene to keep them from trying to exterminate the Talaxians through other means."

"I need to check in with the agency and take my cue

from them. We can't just take matters into our own hands."

"What does your boss think you should do?" she asked.

I held up my com. "I'm having a hard time reaching her. A debris field hit the Krell Satellite. They're making repairs, but until they're finished and it's functional again, I won't be able to find out how she wants to handle this."

"We'll wait, then," she said, climbing onto my lap. "How long do you think it'll be before they fix the satellite?"

"A while. Depends on the damage."

She nodded. "Then we should travel in that direction."

"It'll take us five dias to reach there."

"Perfect." Leaning back in my arms, she smiled up at me. "Once we've arrived, we'll contact your boss, get directions, and then go in and destroy the ray."

"Not *we*."

Her lips twisted. "I want to help. I understand why you don't want to include me on a mission like this. We'd be in danger. But I want someone covering your back."

"That's why Firoh's here."

"Isn't he needed here to run the ship?"

"We could leave you here to run the ground operation," I said, though I doubted she could learn everything she'd need to know before we arrived.

"If you need tractor beam help or someone to fly the craft, I'm afraid that's beyond my abilities. Though I'd love to learn. After we've helped my mom and brought her on board, will you teach me?"

"I'd be glad to, along with weapon's training." I wouldn't always be around to protect her. It was a dangerous world.

She scrambled off my lap. "Why don't you give Firoh the orders, and you can begin my training now?" Her head tilting, she tapped her chin. "Or in a bit."

Because her advice was sound, I gave Firoh the coordinates. Rising, I sauntered around my desk, moving toward her. "Why not start your training right away?" She needed it. Even if I could talk her into remaining on the ship when we put into port at Nebula's Nest, she could still see action. Even a small amount of ability could make the difference.

Taking my hand, she backed toward the bed. "I need you, Matis." Moving into my open arms, she nuzzled my chest. "We don't know what's going to happen next. Taking out what must be a well-guarded device sounds incredibly dangerous. The entire place is probably one big trap. We just found each other. We don't know how long we'll have together."

"You're right, mate," I said, my voice husky with emotion. I lifted her off her feet and lowered her carefully onto the bed, following.

CHAPTER TWENTY-NINE
TATUM

I was not an interstellar agent. He was right that I should remain on board while he completed his mission.

I'd wait to see what his boss suggested. If he was going to be in considerable risk, I wanted to be there to increase his odds of survival.

We lounged in bed after reaffirming our love, but I did need training. Back on Earth, I never thought I'd need to use more than street smarts to survive. I'd relied on my ability to run.

We left his room, and with Snuggles padding behind us, walked to the end of a hall, and took a tiny lift to the lowest level of the ship.

Wearing only a scrap of cloth tied around his waist and between his legs to cover his groin, Matis pretty much made me swoon. And he expected me to be on my toes in a fight? Ha. We'd see.

I checked out his ass as we walked to the training center.

I wanted to tease him about forgetting all about this and returning to bed, but I also wanted to learn as much as I could from him. I didn't know what kind of trouble we might get into soon, but I needed to be as strong and savvy as I could be to defend him. I'd take on an army of Ergeepelon barehanded if that was what I needed to do to protect my mate.

He took me down a final hall to the spaceship's training room that took up almost one half of the ship's lowest level. I stood inside the room, studying the thick plexi mats lining the walls and floor that would provide protection if one of us was thrown in that direction.

Snuggles strolled over to a tiny mattress well out of the way, beside a wall, and climbed onto it, circling before laying down with a sigh and tucking his nose into the fluff of his tail. Naptime for him.

A shooting range took up the left section of the large room. Matis took me there first, handing me a laser gun from a rack.

"Do you know how to load this?" he asked. When I shook my head, he explained, plus showed me the safety and gave me some basic instruction in how to use the mechanical sight and listen to the gun's guidance. "Load it fifty times."

He remained patient while I fumbled around, and even I was shocked by how quickly I could pop out a cartridge and replace it by the time I'd hit fifty.

Stepping within a red half circle, he waved to the screen and tapped a red button on the floor. A soft green band lit up above the screen. "I've armed the training device. We'll begin with simple targets. I want you to keep shooting until you hit the target at least fifty percent of the time."

A moment later, an image of a creature appeared on the screen. Its sickly yellow flesh glowed, and its insides churned darkly beneath its translucent skin. Its knobby head looked comically larger than it's long, skinny body, and it had eight legs.

"Your first of many targets is the abreelar," he said. "Hit the first and two or three more will appear. The computer will learn how you shoot and study your weaknesses, then try to beat you as often as it can."

"Other than somehow destroying the computerized abreelar, how will I know if it's beating me?"

"Pain."

"Oh-kay," I said slowly, unsure what he meant.

"Once you've shown me you can eliminate abreelars at least fifty percent of the time, we'll move to other creatures. Each one moves in a different way."

"I thought you were going to train me with a knife."

"That comes next. A laser is quicker, and you don't need close contact to take out a threat."

"Unless I can throw a knife and hit it."

"Accuracy with a knife takes more practice than we have time for," he said.

I had a feeling shooting with a laser pistol would take

just as much practice, but he was right. At least with a pistol, I'd have a second or two to aim and get off a shot.

"Always study your target," he said. "Note the creature's eight limbs and how it rears back on the two rear legs."

I'd never seen an abreelar before. "Each of the limbs ends with what looks like fluffy tips, not fingers or feet."

"That's how they surprise their victim. An abreelar will shoot each of those fluffy tips at you. They're actually darts coated with a toxin that'll knock you out long enough for the abreelar to strike. You won't wake up in time to defend yourself."

A shudder ripped through me.

"We use this creature for training because you're not only shooting, but also needing to move quickly to avoid the barbs."

"It's not real," I pointed out.

His thick unibrow lifted. "You're correct that this is a simulation. If a barb hits you, it won't knock you out. But it will sting."

"Really?" I frowned at the creature that passively watched us, waiting for us to tell it to engage.

"Really. Each barb will give you a safe taste of what it's like for something to shoot back."

"What are you going to do while I learn how to hit the target fifty percent of the time?"

He grinned. "Watch you."

I huffed. "Maybe you need training too."

He took the gun from me and eased me outside the

red half circle on the floor. "This is the danger zone. Stay outside it unless you want some early training." He tapped his foot on a small black circle on the floor, and lifted his weapon, sighting down it as the abreelar came to life.

Its bright yellow eyes brightened when it saw him, and he started shooting as it appeared to scramble toward him, though I could tell it was still on the screen.

As an interstellar agent, I expected Matis to be a crack shot, so I wasn't surprised.

The abreelar roared and darted side to side to avoid being hit.

He softly squeezed the trigger, and an orange mark blazed on the creature's forehead. It toppled over, "dead" before it hit the rocky soil. A symbol appeared in the upper right corner of the screen, marking his hit.

Before I could suck in a breath, three abreelars raced out from behind a cluster of rocks, roaring as they ran toward him.

I flinched.

With a soft grunt, Matis fired in quick succession. Abreelars dropped quickly, but not before Matis took a few hits. If I didn't see the tiny trickles of blood on his right shoulder and the left side of his naked chest, I'd think he was unscathed.

Two abreelars screeched as they erupted from the ground in the forefront of the screen. They rolled to make themselves smaller targets, but two soft pops sounded in the room and they flopped on the ground. The computer made them disappear.

"Wow," I said, glancing at the corner of the screen. "You didn't miss."

He turned, swiping away the blood on his chest and shoulder. "Lots of practice." He curled a claw my way. "You're up, mate. Let's see what you've got."

CHAPTER THIRTY

MATIS

Tatum had a good eye, a solid grip on the weapon, and an instinct that allowed her to sense the direction the abreelars might appear from next.

"It's going to take me a while to get to fifty percent," she said with a sigh, lowering the weapon after shooting for at least an horus.

"You're improving all the time," I said, stepping into the half circle and tugging her into my arms. "No one does well from the start."

She leaned into my embrace. "How long have you been doing this? Your skill level with the pistol blew me away."

"Twelve yaros. I started my training with the military, then was recruited by Interstellar Interpol. I've been with them since."

She turned in my arms, looking up at me. "Do you like it?"

"I used to."

Her brow furrowed. "Not any longer?"

My huff bled out. "Lately, while I enjoy what I do, it feels hollow." I shrugged. "I'm getting too old for this job. Younger males and females join all the time, and with each yaro, I feel more obsolete."

"You're not *that* old."

"Since I turned thirty-three-yaros, I feel like I am that old. My bones creak, and I worry my reflexes are slowing. It's natural with aging. Sure, I have a lot of good yaros in me still, but how long do I want to keep doing this? Most leave the force by their mid-thirties, and I can see why. They want relationships, families, a life without someone trying to kill them."

"What do *you* want?"

"See, I've been thinking about this over the past few lunar cycles. I own this ship. I could settle in a colony and use the ship for supply runs. That would benefit everyone in the colony." I caught wind with my dream and kept going, my voice lifting with enthusiasm. "There are colonies scattered throughout the galaxy where few ships travel. Not enough profit to make it worth the fuel, but those people need supplies as much as anyone else. Like the new colonies on Merth 4X7 in the Sebula Quadrant. A friend of mine, Kreel, and his mate, Cora, have settled there. Sure, those in the colony are mostly self-sufficient, and they've all purchased synthesizers and fabricators to create the things they can't buy, but they have needs like any other group of people. I could supply those needs at a minimal cost."

"That sounds amazing," she said. "Let's do it."

I blinked. "What?"

"I said, let's do it."

"Just like that, you'd join me on a new adventure?"

"Did we or did we not commit to each other?" she asked in exasperation, though her smile told me she was teasing.

My spine loosened. "We did, didn't we?"

She gave me a nod. "When you told me what you truly do for a living, I wasn't sure where I fit in. As you could see by my shooting abilities, I'm not spy material."

"To be proficient in something like that only takes time and practice. You're already ahead of most recruits."

"You know what I mean. I'm ruthless enough. I'll do almost anything to help my mom. But I'm not sure I could do your job for a living."

I was warming to my colony idea already. "You could be my co-pilot," I said with a grin. "Firoh's quitting soon. He'll disembark when his sons reach the Plushier Space Station." I explained about what happened. "I'll need someone to help fly this craft. If you can cook, all the better, though I'm pretty handy in the galley."

"I can cook." She nibbled on her lower lip. "I don't know how to fly, however."

"I'll teach you all you need to know."

Her arms tightened around me. "Then consider me your co-pilot in training, reporting for duty, sir." She gave me a quick salute.

A feeling of comfort settled around me, making me realize how much I'd longed for a change. I could envision our future running supplies to various colonies.

There were opportunities on Merth 4X7 for new settlers, and I'd love to live close to Kreel. Maybe I could talk my sister and best friend into building a home there themselves. As interstellar detectives, they could travel anywhere, but they'd need a home base.

There were things we needed to settle before this vision could come true though.

I needed to destroy the disintegrator ray. And I needed to give my mate more training.

"How are you with a knife?" I asked.

"You saw and felt my handiwork," she said with a soft laugh. "Not very good. In fact, you were the first person I've ever stabbed, and that was the first time I'd used a knife outside of cutting food."

My heart tightened. We didn't have much time. How was I going to make sure she had enough training to remain safe until this mission was over? I couldn't always be with her to watch out for her.

Was there any place I could leave her until I'd completed the mission? I couldn't think of a drop off point that would be safer than her going with me to the island planet, which was not an option. I'd think about it, see if I could come up with a plan.

If we were anywhere but in this part of the galaxies, I'd consider hiring a bodyguard for her, but there wasn't anyone I trusted in this region.

I took her to the weapon's cabinet, and we selected a few knives she could carry that fit well in her hand and had the right weight for her slighter build and skill level.

We walked over to one of the mats.

"One thing to always remember," I said, "is to avoid conflict as much as you can."

She nodded, staring at the knife in my hand.

"If there's a nonviolent way to resolve a situation, take it."

"Do you think that exists on Nebula's Nest?"

I shrugged. "I don't plan for you to find out. I want you to remain on the ship while Firoh and I continue this mission, but just in case, I wanted to mention it. You may find yourself in a tenuous situation in the future. It's worth pointing it out."

She nodded, watching as I shifted back and forth on the mat.

"Basic tips. Keep your knife close to your body and close to your dominant hand. This will help you move quickly and keep your opponent from taking your knife away."

"I'll remember."

"Use quick, sharp movements to slash at your opponent. The goal is to cause as much damage as possible so you can run away." I didn't want to think of her in a situation where she'd have to use a knife. She was small compared to most aliens, and incredibly vulnerable. "Don't let bravery be your downfall."

"Yeah, I see what you're saying. I tend to jump into things without worrying about the consequences. Like coming here."

After laying the knife by my feet, I tugged her into my arms for a quick hug. "If you hadn't, we wouldn't have met, and I can't imagine anything worse than that."

She chuckled. "You're right. Despite our shaky start, this is the best thing that's ever happened to me."

We parted, and I lifted the knife again, continuing my instruction, including showing her some simple blocks.

"Pay attention to your surroundings," I said. "Use them to your advantage. For example, if there is a container or boulder nearby, you can use it for cover. Always assume the other person is trying to hurt you and react accordingly." I caught her eye. "I'm going to attack you in slow motion. Use one of the simple moves I just taught you to block the blow."

I moved toward her, exaggerating the movement, and she did a decent job of deflecting my attack. Before I could slow-lunge again, she rolled, coming up behind me.

"Assume there's a chair or something between us," she said. "I put myself behind it."

"Good," I said. "That's what you need to do."

We worked throughout the afternoon, finally returning to my cabin.

"I'm wiped out," she said, collapsing on the bed.

"I'll go fetch water for the tub."

"We could use the cleansing unit." Sitting up, she dropped her legs over the edge of the bed. "It takes buckets and buckets of water and a lot of physical effort to fill that tub, let me tell you."

"But if we use the cleansing unit, we can't fit inside together. The tub is bigger."

Her eyes lit up. "Ohhh."

"Exactly." I crossed the room and bent over to kiss her. "Wait here and as soon as the tub is full, it's my turn to wash *your* back."

CHAPTER THIRTY-ONE

TATUM

We returned to the training room each dia. He walked. I hobbled until he scooped me up and carried me.

"If I can't move," I said with a groan. "How am I going to defend myself?"

"We'll stretch first. That'll help."

Inside the training room, he put me through a series of moves that loosened my muscles. After, I still ached, but at least I didn't wince with every step.

On the fifth dia, with our arrival at Nebula's Nest looming, we trained again. The fifty percent score eluded me, though I'd made progress each dia. On day four, I'd scored a forty-five, my best so far.

"Here's your gun," he said, handing it over on dia five. "Today, we'll mix it up."

"No more abreelars?"

"You've graduated from abreelars."

"But I haven't hit them fifty percent of the time," I

said, squinting at the screen. As a competitive person, I wanted to win this, even if it was only a simulation.

"Today, I want you to try a city visual. Your targets will vary, and one of the keys here is to shoot only those dressed in red. Avoid anyone in blue."

I frowned. "Why blue?"

"They're civilians."

"I'm not shooting kids."

"What if one of them is running at you with a knife?" He watched my face. Was this a test?

"You said to avoid conflict wherever possible. If a child comes at me with a knife, I'll run, hide, whatever is needed, but if I can't evade the kid, I'll block blows and try to disarm them."

He nodded, then programmed the screen. A cityscape appeared with partly collapsed buildings and burned vehicles crashed on the rutted street. A fake wind whistled through the buildings, and bangs rang out here and there.

"Let's see how you score today," he said.

I stood within the red circle and waited with the weapon ready. In no time, a big, four-limbed alien of a species I'd never seen before lumbered into view holding a laser blaster. It pointed the weapon my way, and I took careful aim and squeezed the trigger, hitting the creature before it could send a dart toward me.

Three more of the same species raced from various locations, each shooting at me. I was only able to take out one before the others hit me with darts, but I eliminated them not long after that.

Adrenaline blazed through my veins, making my heart race and my hands shake.

At one point, five aliens rushed at me all at once. I crouched, shooting and moving around within the half circle, avoiding their barbs.

By the time the session had ended, I could barely stand, and my body was a mass of shakes from being hit by the barbs and the effort I'd made to remain safe.

"Well done," Matis said, taking the gun from my trembling hand. "Very well done. Sixty percent. You've passed quickly. Do you know how long it takes most recruits to achieve a sixty percent score?"

"Six dias?" I said with a smirk.

He placed the laser gun on a nearby shelf and scooped me up, taking me to the mat, where he laid me on the rubbery surface.

"You're amazing," he said. "You've trained so hard, never complaining."

"I moan and groan a lot." And I'd taken a lot of baths, soaking until the water chilled.

"I have a reward for you," he said, his eyes sparkling.

My pulse picked up, and anticipation flowed through me like warm honig. "I do love rewards."

"Computer?" he called out. "Lock the door."

A click echoed in the room.

Matis peeled off my clothing and proceeded to massage my entire body, starting at my feet and slowly working his way to the top of my head. He gently rolled me onto my belly and gave my backside the same luscious treatment as he'd given my front.

By the time he'd finished, I was a moaning wreck and not only relaxed, but completely on fire for him.

"If you don't fuck me, I'm going to scream at you," I said, peeking at him over my shoulder.

He grinned. Rising, he shucked his training garment, displaying his stiff cock. He dropped over me. "You're going to scream, mate, but for a completely different reason." Parting my legs, he lifted my hips and centered the head of his cock at my dripping core.

One thrust, and he embedded himself deep inside me.

I moaned.

"That's not a scream, mate," he said with a laugh. "Let me see what I can do to make sure you're truly into this."

Oh, fuck.

There was nothing I could do but lie there and enjoy the ride.

And, yes, by the time he was finished, I'd screamed more than once.

CHAPTER THIRTY-TWO

MATIS

I rose before Tatum the next dia, dressed quickly, and slipped from the room, striding to the bridge, where I sat in the empty seat beside Firoh.

He startled awake, dropping his heels off the dash, clunking them on the floor. "Sorry," he mumbled, scrubbing his silver hair off his face. He secured it at his nape and turned to face me, rubbing his right thigh where he'd sustained the most injuries. "I must've fallen asleep."

"You need it," I said, not a bit disturbed. Despite me relieving him on the bridge half the night shifts during our travels, he'd been pulling long horuses since we left the Weldroolar Space Station.

"Before we approached the island a few horuses ago," he said, "I cloaked the ship. We're orbiting now. They don't know we're here, but I wouldn't trust that for long."

"Any news from the agency?"

He tapped on the hover screen beside him. "Looks like they should be finished with repairs on satellite soon. I put a ping out. When a signal can go through, I'll be notified. I'm sure we'll hear back quickly once it's fully functional. I'll put the call through to your com the secunda it comes through."

"I appreciate it." Leaning back, I kicked my feet up on the dash. "Any news about your sons?"

"Yeah." A long pause followed while he studied his claws. About my build, Firoh had dark purple skin common among his Chullod people. He was an amazing pilot and a good person. I'd miss him once he left the agency.

"Will they be there soon?" I asked.

"They've arrived on the Plushier Space Station." His pale purple eyes darted away from mine, telling me he hated to leave me in the middle of an assignment. If anything, he'd been more determined to perform the best job possible since his injury.

"We need to send you to them, then," I said. Those younglings needed him desperately. He was all the family they had left. I'd never hold him back from something like that.

"I'll get to them soon enough. They're safe where they are."

He was not safe with me.

As pirates, we'd be welcome to put into any port and visit the town. I could off-load my cargo and take on a new one if I chose. But if the disintegrator ray was being constructed inside that warehouse, I was going to blow it into such tiny bits, they'd be combing the outer galaxy to find them. Bombing it was the only thing I could think of doing, though I'd also steal a few vital components and ensure the agency hid them forever, including the one in my safe.

Pirates never took the betrayal of one of their own kind well. We'd be wanted males once the explosion went off.

Firoh couldn't get further involved in this. I wouldn't risk his life when he was all the younglings had left.

"As soon as I hear from the agency," I said, "I want you to buy a small ship and head to the space station. I'll make sure the necessary credits are in your account." Lifting my com, I started the transaction.

"I don't need credits. You know my family's incredibly wealthy."

Him, too.

"I can't leave until this job is done," he said. "You need me as back-up."

"I've got Tatum."

"You think she'll be any good in a fight?" Firoh snorted. "A cabin boy who I note is *not* a boy is not much of a back-up."

"I've been working with her, but I won't take her to the island. She'll remain here and provide cover for the ship."

"Then you have a plan for Nebula's Nest."

"If the agency can't give me better options, I'm going down there. If I find the ray, I'll make sure it's destroyed."

"We've worked on this job for many lunar cycles. I want to be a part of the finish."

"Which is why I'm going down to Nebula's Nest with Matis," Tatum said from behind us. She strolled onto the bridge in complete badass mode from the weapons strapped all over her person to the flinty gleam in her eyes. "I know you want me to remain here, Matis, but it makes more sense for me to go with you and for Firoh to stay back on the ship. One, he knows how to use your tractor beam, or whatever you call it. Two, he knows how to run the ship. And three, he needs to collect those younglings and give them a home."

"Absolutely not," I said at the same time as Firoh.

He stood and turned to face her. "You're not even an agent."

She strode right up to him and while he didn't gulp, his gaze did glide down her frame appreciatively.

I growled.

Color rose into his face, and his hands swung wide. "Didn't mean anything by it."

I growled again for good measure and stood. "You're not going with me, Tatum."

She huffed. "You can't stop me."

I prepared myself to grab her. I'd haul her to our cabin and lock her inside with Snuggles.

A ping rang out from the dash.

"That's the agency," Firoh said, sending a knowing look between me and Tatum. "Do you want to take it now or somewhere private?"

"Here," I grunted. I shot Tatum a stern look. "Go to

our cabin." And because I could understand why she was so determined to come with me, I lowered my voice. "Please."

She leaned against the wall and crossed her arms over her chest. "No."

CHAPTER THIRTY-THREE
TATUM

He wasn't going to play he-alien on me now. He'd trained me for days, and while I wasn't much of a fighter, I could be of use. More so on the island than stuck on the ship with my finger hovering over the tractor beam button.

I realized it was going to take some persuasion on my part to convince him.

He lifted his com and waved at me with his other arm as if he wanted me to leave the bridge.

No way. I might not be an employee of the agency, but I had a stake in this. Matis was mine, and I was going to protect him.

With a roll of his eyes, Matis took the call. Firoh, the big dark purple guy, snorted and settled in the captain's chair, hooking his right leg carefully over the arm. Matis had mentioned a grave injury three yaros ago that Firoh had overcome and performed as well, if not better, than any other within the agency.

Firoh's lips quirked up. He watched us like this was a sporting event and we were evenly matched. I respected him for that.

"Yes?" Matis said into his com.

"I understand you have good news for us," a female said, her voice tinny, indicating the call traveled a long distance to reach us.

Matis explained about what we'd found in the statue, plus the details he'd already shared related to the Vessar who'd died to get the island's schematic and information to him.

"I was hoping you'd have some agents in the area who could lend a claw," Matis said.

"I'm afraid we don't. The Vessars are up to their old tricks, or should I say new ones. We had two agents in your area, but we had to pull them for a different job."

"I'll go in and handle it, then," Matis said without a hint of inflection.

"You've got Firoh, correct?"

"Yup."

"Will that be enough?"

"We can handle it." His gaze met mine, and his lips thinned. "I also have a new recruit I can deputize."

Ha. My spine tightened, and I shot him a grin. The crystal in my pocket hummed, and I sensed approval of the plan, which made my body stop twitching.

"See it done, then," she said. "I'm sorry I can't help further. You know how it is. Budget cuts everywhere. It's all I can do to keep this place running."

Even for something like this? But then, we needed to

act, not wait until she could send help. Who knows how long that might take?

"I understand," he said. "I'll report once this is over."

"Very well."

He tapped on his com. "Just sent a brief summary. Take a quick look."

Silence echoed in the room, followed by her sharp inhale. "Well, isn't that interesting?"

"Any restrictions you want to impose on this job?" he asked.

"There's no way I could, Matis," she said, sounding stunned. "Do whatever you need to do. You don't need my permission with something like this." She sighed. "I'm *truly* sorry I can't send other agents in. Wow. This is something else. I commend you for what you've done so far, and I'm grateful you're the one handling this part of the mission."

"Thanks. We'll . . . need to talk when I get back."

"I had a feeling you might want a conversation."

His gaze met mine. "I've met someone. I want to be with her."

Firoh's nod showed his approval. He was a nice guy. I hoped things worked out with his sons.

"We'll support you no matter what you choose to do," the woman said. "You know that. But . . . we'll miss you."

They ended the call.

I liked that he'd claimed me, that he'd spoken well of me to his boss, and that he saw us together for the long haul. I felt the same. A nice life in a colony with supply runs here and there sounded like an amazing future for us.

"So, I'll remain on the ship," Firoh said, rubbing his right thigh.

"You know I'm not going to risk you."

Firoh's chin lifted and pride shined in his eyes. "You know I can handle anything."

"There's no one else I'd rather have beside me on an assignment. But Tatum is right. We don't have time to teach her how to run the ship or engage the extractor beams. Even if we'd started training her dias ago, she wouldn't be ready. Anything could go wrong, and we need the ship to escape to."

He grumbled.

I held in my grin, though it faded fast. This wasn't going to be a party. We'd be in considerable danger. I still didn't know how Matis planned to destroy the ray, assuming we found it inside the warehouse. And if we did, they'd hunt us. We'd need to act and get out of there fast. If they caught us, they'd kill us.

"We leave in ten minue," Matis said, looking me over. "You need to be less obvious."

I glanced down at the "pirate" costume I'd concocted back in his room, using some of his clothing I'd taken a quick stitching to.

"I look good." I said.

"Obviously," Firoh agreed with a chuckle. His gaze shot between us. "So, the cabin boy who is not a boy is now..."

"Mine," Matis growled.

"I have no interest in poaching," Firoh said, still laughing. He sobered, nodding to Matis. "I don't like that you feel I should remain here, but I appreciate it." His gaze swept in my direction. "You two will need all the help you can get, and I'll do my part on the ship."

"Let's go," Matis said, taking my arm as he passed me. "We need to get down to the planet and find out if they're rebuilding that ray."

CHAPTER THIRTY-FOUR

MATIS

I packed a bag in our room, raiding the supply closet in the hall.

"I still want you to remain here," I said. "Though I know you won't agree."

"Nope," she said, bracing herself for an argument.

"You'd be safer here, and I can handle this myself."

"I heard your boss," she said. "She's worried about you doing this without back-up. I'll help all I can. I'll protect you."

"I love you, mate," I said softly.

She blinked fast. "Yup. Me too."

Snuggles leapt from the bed onto my shoulder, but I gently tugged him off. I held him in my arms like a youngling, rubbing his belly while he purred.

"You need to stay here, little guy," I said. I couldn't risk him too. I laid him on the bed and he snarled, suspecting I was going to trap him inside my cabin.

"Ready?" I asked Tatum, and she gave me a sharp

nod. Her hand remained on the hilt of the laser pistol she'd donned, and I was grateful we'd taken the time to give her training. She would be considered a very raw recruit, but at least she wasn't defenseless.

I lifted my wrist and hailed Firoh. "Ready."

"Alright. Give me a secunda."

"You'll keep a solid lock on us at all times," I growled.

"Of course. In and out."

"He'll drop us near the port," I told Tatum. "We'll make our way to the warehouse on foot."

She nodded and came over to stand close to me.

If only there was time for one last kiss. One last bout in bed. A chance to show her what she meant to me. We'd take care while on the island, but anything could happen.

"Once we're in port, I can't hold you or show you what you mean to me," I said, my voice croaking with emotion. I tugged her into my arms. "Down there, you'll be my cabin boy again. If I show deference to you, someone will suspect something is up."

"Maybe they'll think your cabin boy warms your bed," she said with a soft laugh.

"Stay close. Don't do anything risky."

She nodded and stepped away from me. "I don't want you doing anything risky either."

As we were beamed to the surface, I grunted. She should know I'd risk everything to keep her safe.

CHAPTER THIRTY-FIVE
TATUM

One secunda, we stood in Matis's cabin, the next, on a broad loading dock behind a line of huge metal containers.

I was surprised by a variety of things. Fresh air where I'd thought it would smell canned. Sunshine warming my face.

And the lack of people.

A few aliens puttered about, loading one container or another, but I'd braced myself for loads of alien pirates striding around. I thought they'd grab us. Question us. Instead, it appeared no one noticed we'd appeared, and if they did, they didn't care.

We moved away from the dock and onto a street heading toward town, our eyes peeled for any sign of danger. Thick, humid air surrounded us, and the stench of sweat and spent fuel clung to my sinuses. It was all I could do to take in the sights, sounds, and smells unlike any I'd experienced before.

As we got closer to town, aliens of all shapes, sizes, and colors shuffled along with us, most heading in our direction. A few passed us, aiming for the port. Some of the aliens had two arms and legs like us, while others had multiple heads atop their humanoid bodies. A few had antennae instead of ears and tails of various lengths and thicknesses. Some were dressed in brightly colored outfits, making me think they could be traders or entertainers.

As we approached the main section of the town, pirates weren't just on the streets. Some stood above us on rooftops like vultures waiting to swoop down at any moment. Even though an intense buzz came from all around us as people went about their tasks, it felt like many were waiting, though I couldn't determine what they anticipated happening.

The buildings were universally gray and rundown, but I assumed with such a small area, they couldn't fabricate construction materials. Everything would need to be brought to the planet and at considerable cost. Other than a few buildings that looked like two-story inns, the rest were single-story dwellings or hovels with tables set up in front for vendors to hawk their wares.

We came to an intersection of a road encircling the small town. The path we'd taken from the port continued through the center, and I spied an open area ahead that appeared to house a market.

"Where's the warehouse?" I whispered to Matis, carefully peering around. I injected swagger into my stride and did my best to suck in my chest and appear like a teenage male.

"This way." Shifting the pack on his shoulder, he turned left and started down the road meandering around the back side of town.

I spied a large building ahead. "How are we going to do this?"

He paused in the shadow of a dingy building and stared at the single-story warehouse. "It's heavily guarded, as expected."

We needed to get inside without being seen. How were we going to do that?

I casually looked in that direction, taking in the lack of viewing ports on the walls and the mix of armed, six-limbed Ergeepelons patrolling around the building.

"From the top?" I asked. I picked up a rock and drew in the dirt by my feet, pretending I was passing the time while we sat. "A distraction might come in handy."

"Yes," he said slowly. He leaned his head back against the building and closed his eyes, pretending he planned to take a nice nap.

"Could Firoh help?" I asked, meaning transport us inside now that we had general coordinates. In case anyone was listening, we needed to keep our conversation generic.

"Too risky," he said. "Wouldn't want to pop inside a metal device or next to someone who'd be angry we appeared."

"Delivery service or maintenance crew?"

"They'd suspect something underhanded."

Right, pirates. "Distraction may be our best bet, then."

"Agreed." He lumbered to his feet and held a hand out to me, tugging me up beside him. "Let's get something to eat." Turning, he strolled toward the warehouse, pausing at a two-story building beside it with a sign swaying out front, *Cosmic Cutthroat*. Lovely name right there.

We went inside and dropped onto stools at a table on the left side of the room conveniently next to a porthole looking out at the warehouse. Matis lowered his bag to the floor between his boots.

An alien strolled out from behind the bar and sauntered toward us. Tall and slender, she had a sleek, angular frame. Her scaled skin shimmered metallic silver and a mane of iridescent, writhing tentacles crowned her head.

"What can I get you?" she asked in a low, sultry voice. Her smile revealed a row of sharp, jagged pink teeth. Her attention remained on Matis. She'd dismissed me already, and I wasn't sure if I should be miffed or grateful.

A list of drinks hovered in front of us, and I squinted, trying to read the choices.

"Whiskey," Matis said.

The bartender nodded, and her gaze finally fell on me. One of her silver brows lifted. "Foogar milk, youngling?"

"I'll have the . . . Cosmic Cocktail," I said. Must be a signature drink.

The bartender's other eyebrow lifted to join the first, and she shot Matis a look I couldn't discern.

He nodded, and she pivoted and strutted back to the bar.

"I don't intend to drink it," I said defensively. "Jeez, foogar milk. Really?"

He snorted. "She thinks you're a youngling, which is our intention."

"And who are you, my father?"

"Anything but." He leaned close to whisper. "But if you want to call me daddy later, I'll be happy to tell you you're a good girl."

My pulse rocketed to the moon orbiting the island. "I could dress up," I said softly. "Any suggestions?"

His eyes smoldered. "You are a distraction."

Satisfied I'd made his heartrate pick up, I leaned back against the wall and surveyed the bar, my gaze skimming over various aliens before I casually peered out the porthole.

Ah. Interesting.

I tapped his thigh, and his gaze zoned in on me. I could tell he was still thinking about the daddy/good girl comment and not focused on our task at hand. When I twitched my shoulder toward the porthole, his eyes hardened, and he peered in that direction.

He slowly nodded. "It might work."

We didn't have any other options.

As the bartender lowered our drinks onto the plexi table, I studied the warehouse. A large air vent projected from near the edge of the roof, jutting downward, and I suspected we might be able to stuff ourselves inside it and find a way into the building.

All we needed to do was avoid being seen by the Ergeepelons patrolling this side of the building.

And that's when I came up with the perfect distraction.

CHAPTER THIRTY-SIX

MATIS

"Your idea is bold," I said softly once we stood outside the bar. I'd taken a few sips of my drink, as had Tatum, then dumped the rest on the floor when no one was looking. We paid and left. Now we slumped against the outer wall of the Cosmic Cutthroat, me with my bag on the ground beside my boots. "If they retaliate, Firoh will be dead before we blink, and we'll no longer have a way out of here."

"Too bad we can't deflect the shot so it appears to come from a different direction."

"That wouldn't work. In fact . . . "Hold on. Frowning, I thought about it before nudging her shoulder. "What an amazing idea."

She beamed. "See? I do come in handy for more than daddy play."

"Would you really consider daddy play?"

Her expression went contemplative. "Maybe."

Now was not a good time to get an erection. I shook

the idea off, though it wasn't easy, and thought about the proposed distraction. It would be best to get Firoh's input.

She tapped her pocket. "If it helps you feel better, my little friend here is humming happily, indicating she likes this idea."

"How do you know it's female?"

"What else would she be?"

I shook my head. We could talk about that later.

After strolling around to make sure no one was near enough to overhear, I sat on the ground, closed my eyes, and leaned against the building as if I'd decided to slumber the dia away. After a few secunda, I added a few snores and slumped against Tatum, grateful she was playing along. Turning, I place my head on her shoulder and carefully lifted my wrist com to speak.

I kept my voice low. "Firoh."

"Yes?" he quietly asked.

I introduced the idea.

"I'll be happy to blow up anything," he said. "But what's keeping them from shooting back?"

I explained.

"I've got a better idea," he said. "What do you think about cloaked drones?"

Yes. "Perfect. Could you arrange for this within the next few minues?"

"Certainly, boss. On it."

He cut out, and I lowered my arm, whispering to Tatum. "Are you ready to run for that air vent?"

She nodded and shot me a feral grin.

Appearing as if I'd ended my nap and had to pee, I stood and sauntered around to the back of the inn, leaving Tatum to guard my bag. After fumbling with the front of my pants a bit, I returned to Tatum and slouched against the building.

A lone Vessar cut onto the road looping around the town, stomping in our direction.

Tatum hissed and slunk against the inn.

I held back my grin. Vessars rarely went anywhere alone, which could be why my contact had been so easily targeted.

"Firoh sent a friend," I said softly.

"Ah. Wonderful." She frowned at the "Vessar" who was actually the cloaked drone.

"I believe it's in our best interest to put some distance between us and it," I said. "Perhaps we should meander in another direction?" Acting drunk, I staggered down the street, barely avoiding bumping into the Vessar, who snarled quite realistically. Tatum grabbed my arm and put it around her shoulder, adding to the impression I needed support.

We made our way around the back of the inn and headed in the general direction of the air vent.

We'd just taken a spot behind an abandoned building within view of the vent when the drone disguised as a Vessar began firing.

CHAPTER THIRTY-SEVEN

TATUM

The Ergeepelon guards shouted and raced toward the front of the building, their weapons lifted. After making sure no one was watching, we ran toward the vent.

When we reached it, Matis didn't hesitate. He stuffed me up inside and quickly followed, dragging his bag as we crawled up the narrow metal structure until we reached the top. There, we moved forward toward a screen blocking our entrance into the warehouse.

There wasn't room for both of us inside the tight vent; I lay on my belly hoping my feet didn't stick out the bottom with him pretty much lying on top of me.

"Well, that settles it," he said softly, pointing. "That's the ray."

The enormous ray took up most of the open warehouse. It was a towering strturcture surrounded by a tangle of pipes, wires, and various other technical components. At its core, I spied a glowing, pulsating orb of energy, surrounded by a series of powerful electro-magnets and what I assumed were laser emitters.

"How can you be sure?" I whispered.

"I've seen drawings."

More information from contacts? I wouldn't keep talking and risk exposure.

Ergeepelon workers scrambled about the warehouse, assembling the various components and adding a thick, armored shell to the structure, likely so it could withstand the intense energy of the ray's discharge. The air buzzed and the sharp, electric smell of ozone drifted our way.

Thousands of parts. I bet they'd found most of what they need. For all we knew, the part we'd found was all they were missing to complete the ray. If they could fabricate that single component, they would've. But the Ergeepelon who'd hired me wouldn't have sent me after the statue if there was another way.

"We can't let them complete the device," Matis said.

It would be capable of disintegrating buildings, vehicles, and even entire planets with a single shot. And they'd fire it on the peaceful Talaxians.

Hints of danger lurked within the warehouse. The workers moved with a sense of urgency, as if they were racing against some unseen clock. And while the ray might be a marvel of science and technology, something many scientists would ache to study, it needed to be destroyed forever.

"I'll plant the explosives as close to the device's base as possible," he said by my ear.

I turned my head so he could hear my barely there whisper. "How will we do that unseen?"

"Not we," he said. "Me. I want you to wait here."

"I'll go in with you as cover."

"You can cover me from here." He pulled a tool from his bag and started working on the grate, taking care not to make a sound as he loosened it from the wall.

The workers never looked in our direction, but that didn't mean they wouldn't see Matis slipping from the opening and into the room.

"We need another distraction, and fast." The commotion out front had gone silent, telling me the Ergeepelons had destroyed the droid. They'd suspect something was going on and ensure the ray was safe.

"You are not going to risk yourself," he said.

"Another droid?"

"I doubt it'll work a second time."

"Then maybe Firoh needs to blast something bigger and do so from the cloaked ship." The crystal hummed in agreement.

"Yeah," he said, lifting his wrist, speaking softly. "Firoh?"

"Yes, boss?" Firoh whispered.

"Can you create an enormous distraction? The droid worked, but it isn't enough. We've got a live one here, and it's time to end its existence."

"On it."

Firoh had barely ended the call when the front of the warehouse exploded. Ergeepelon workers jumped and raced toward that side of the building.

"Cover me," Matis hissed, ripping off the grate and leaning it against the side of the air vent. He scrambled out of the hole, jumping with the bag of explosives in hand. Now would not be a good time for him to take enemy fire.

I sheltered within the metal tunnel with my laser gun poised to fire. Matis raced to the back of the device, quickly disappearing from view.

The workers milled around the crumbled opening at the front of the warehouse. None cried out or rushed Matis's way, and I started to think this just might work out like it should.

A hover car zipped close and settled on the ground in front of the collapsed wall. The hatch opened, and the Ergeepelon who'd hired me scrambled out of the vehicle.

"Secure the device," he bellowed, waving his limbs toward the cratered warehouse front. "Fix this now. Cover it up. Do what you need to do to mask this!"

My pulse thundered so loud in my ears; I swore Firoh would be able to hear it on the ship.

I waited, tense and with sweaty palms for Matis to reappear, though now I worried he'd be seen making his way back to me.

There was no way I could wait here and watch him rush across the open side of the warehouse and jump back into the vent to join me. There were too many Ergeepelon in the front of the building for him to risk being out in the open. He'd be seen no matter what he did.

Since no one appeared to be looking my way, I

dropped my legs into the big room and jumped, landing hard on the plexi floor. Without waiting for shouts or laser shots aimed my way, I raced along the wall toward the back of the device.

Behind it, I slammed into Matis.

"Tatum," he said, his gaze frantic. He latched onto my arms. "I told you to wait in the vent."

Shouts rang out from the front of the warehouse, and Matis's panicked gaze met mine.

The crystal in my pocket released a shrill string of notes, suggesting my spine was about to be severed. I could almost feel the bead of the laser gun sighting in on us.

Heavy footsteps rushed in our direction.

My heart slammed up into my throat, and I cringed, though that wouldn't keep me from being killed.

"Firoh?" Matis snarled into his com. "Get us out of here!"

CHAPTER THIRTY-EIGHT

MATIS

A pop, and we stood on the bridge once more.

Tatum pawed her body and then mine. "No wounds. No wounds!"

"I'm all right," I said, gripping her upper arms to hold her steady. When she ran into me, my heart essentially stopped. All I could think about was protecting her, getting her out of that trap.

I hauled her into my arms and held her tight enough she squeaked. Then I lifted her and seared her mouth with my kiss.

"Uh, boss?" Firoh's urgent voice cut through the minue I'd wanted to savor with the knowledge that we were safe for now. "Boss!"

As torturous as it was, I stopped kissing Tatum, lowering her to her feet, though I kept a hold of her hand.

"Yeah," I snarled. I mean, I wanted to keep kissing her. No, I wanted to take her to our cabin and make sure she felt safe and completely loved. I needed to reaffirm out bond.

"Want to watch the action on the island?" Firoh crowed, and a holoimage of the warehouse lit up above his viewscreen.

I'd set the timer for a tight window, and it wasn't long before we were rewarded with an enormous explosion.

It leveled the warehouse. Flames shot toward the sky, and aliens of various shapes and sizes fled the scene, racing for the port to escape in their ships.

"Oh, shit," Firoh shouted, his glee falling away from his face. He stared at the flashing lights on the notifier screen. "Our cloaking device has been penetrated. Incoming. Hold on!"

I sunk into the second chair and dragged Tatum onto my lap, pinning us down with my crossed arms and hands latched onto the armrests.

The ship shuddered, and alarms blared.

"Get us out of here, Firoh," I growled.

"What, you don't want to hang around Nebula's Nest for a bit longer?" Firoh asked, though his hands flew across the controls. "Maybe get another drink at the Cosmic Cutthroat?"

Tatum squeaked and slapped her hand over her right pants pocket. "We can't stay here! The crystal is humming up a discordant storm. Get out of here or we're going splat!"

"Chart a course to anywhere but here, Firoh, and do it now," I bellowed.

He shot me a roll of his eyes. "Do you truly think I want to hang around here, waiting for them to show us how pissed off they are?"

Another blast hit the ship, but so far, the hull appeared to be intact. We'd find out how extensive the damage was when we'd escaped this quadrant and could put into a neutral port to assess the hull.

"Engaging thrusters and . . ." Firoh compressed a lever on the dash. "Go!"

Outside the plexi viewscreen, the stars blurred. The ship's thrusters roared. We blasted back against our seats.

The hull shuddered but held. Tatum clung to my arms, whimpering, and Snuggles bounded from the hall behind us and launched himself onto my shoulder. He held on as the ship rocked and slammed, taking us to safety.

As quickly as the sounds lifted, silence descended.

The ship leveled, and the sirens stopped blaring. Flashing lights overhead winked out.

Only the sound of our breathing echoed on the bridge.

Firoh slumped back in his chair and a laugh burst from him. "I tell ya, boss. When you decide to give a guy a send-off, you sure do it in style."

CHAPTER THIRTY-NINE

TATUM

While Matis updated the agency, I took Snuggles to our cabin. The space kitty rode on my shoulder, rubbing his head against mine, purring up a storm. I think we were friends now.

I dropped him on the bed and contemplated the room we'd call home during future supply runs.

They say home is where the heart is.

Mine was wherever Matis laid his head. I could understand his eagerness to settle in one place, to build something permanent he could call his own, and to develop friendships with neighbors. I was excited to hear more about the colony he'd mentioned. Only Mom kept me on Earth. With all the adventure I'd had on this trip, I couldn't imagine returning to my old life and job. The stars were out here, and I couldn't wait to see them all.

"Who's been a good girl?" Matis said from the open doorway. He crossed his arms over his chest and tried to look stern.

"Me. I've been good," I said, playing along with the made-up daddy-good girl roles we'd teased each other about. We hadn't discussed where this might go, but he wasn't the dominant type. I could be bratty, however, and I thrived while behaving in that manner. So, because I enjoyed being a total witch, I tapped my chin and frowned. "Or maybe I *haven't* been good enough. I believe I've been quite naughty."

Heat coiled inside me, a taut spring about to snap.

Snuggles, sensing upcoming action, snarled and raced for the bathroom. I sauntered over and shut the door. No need for interruptions.

Matis entered the room and closed the panel behind him. "I believe it's time you showed me how good you can be, *cabin girl.*"

"Watch me." I strode over to him and started undoing the fastenings on his shirt. I spread the fabric, revealing his muscular chest. When I touched him, he groaned. Now this was going to be fun. "Is this good?"

He struggled to frown. "Not quite good enough, I'd say. What else have you got?"

I smiled playfully and let my fingertips wander across his body, exploring every contour and ripple of muscle beneath his skin. His breathing deepened as I moved up, lightly scratching him with my nails before making my way back down again. His pleasure was like an electric current running through him, heating up the surrounding air until I could almost taste it.

I reached for the fastener of his pants and undid it, spreading the material apart. When I looked into his eyes to see if he wanted more, he jerked out a nod and ran his fingers through my hair, taking care with his claws. Shivers tracked down my spine. With gentle pressure on the back of my neck, he guided me closer to his engorged cock.

My heart thumped heavily as I kissed the tip of his thick length. It surged upward, straining toward me.

Shifting positions, we tore at each other's clothing until we were completely naked.

"Love you," I whispered. He was my alien ogre, and I adored him from the top of his head to his big, clawed toes. There wasn't anything I wouldn't do to make him happy.

"Our daddy-good girl act is dissolving," he said softly. "I love you too."

"Love is good." It was pure and wonderful, and it would keep growing between us.

"It sure is."

"As is this." I took him into my mouth with care, swirling my tongue around the head of his cock before gliding my lips down. I couldn't take him all; he was much too big, but I could still bring him joy.

I loved the feel of my lips and tongue sliding over his hot skin, plus the way his breathing hitched when I ran a fingertip along the underside of his shaft. I cupped his balls, rolling them, and he groaned, pushing forward to meet me in deep thrusts.

He tightened his grip on my hair, holding me close as I worked him harder and faster, licking and sucking and caressing every inch of him, driving him onward until he teetered on the edge.

With a hoarse cry, he pulled away from me. He turned me around so my back was to him and bent me forward.

"You're good. So very good." He braced my hips and nudged the head of his shaft inside me.

"Show me," I said, thrusting myself back to meet the tip of his cock.

He drove himself into me. I moaned as his large cock stretched me almost painfully, the dull ache mixing with fire running through my veins.

"Is this good?" he growled. Each of his powerful strokes sending blasts of heat through me. "Or this?" His hands roamed over my body as he moved, caressing my breasts and finding my clit to stroke it in time with his driving force.

He kept shoving into me, burying himself completely. The ridges along the length of his cock caressed my inner walls.

Pleasure built inside me until I was screaming out his name, attempting to push back against the orgasm roaring like a spaceship hurtling through a wormhole. It consumed me just as Matis claimed everything that was me. I gave to him freely, savoring how wonderful it was to feel so complete.

I shuddered with pleasure while he flicked his thumb across my clit as if to remind me of where this was coming from. Only he fit with me so perfectly. Only with him would I ever feel complete.

Holding my hips with one hand, his other rolling my clit, he started going faster, pushing harder. I gasped for breath as another powerful orgasm started building within me.

I cried out in delight at the intense spasms rocked through my body like a wave, crashing through me over and over until I thought I'd die from the heady sensations.

Leaning over me, he nibbled where my shoulder met my neck, biting down gently while he continued to thrust his cock deep within me.

Another orgasm rocketed through my body, and my hoarse cry echoed in the room.

He shuddered above me, overcome with his own pleasure, pushing forward hard. Heat filled me as he gave way, bathing my inner walls with his essence. His pace slowed, though he continued to move within me, pushing me into an orgasm once more with strokes of my clit.

When I felt like I couldn't take any more, he pulled out of me. He lifted me and gently laid me on the bed, joining me. Curling around me, he held me.

He stroked my body and murmured in my ear. "You're a very good girl."

I kissed his arm. "And you're a good boy."

His chuckle rang out. "Somehow, good boy doesn't have quite the same ring to it."

"But you're good," I said, using his words. "Very good."

His arms tightened around me. "We're right for each other. You bring out my best and make me realize even my worst is enough."

I rolled over to face him and kissed him, lingering on his mouth. I couldn't breathe if we weren't connected.

"Boss?" Firoh called out through Matis's wrist com.

Matis scowled. "Should I ignore him or . . .?"

"Find out what he needs, and then you can be a good boy again."

His grin took over his face and made his eyes sparkle. "Perhaps being a good boy has its merits."

"Very much so," I said, grinning right back at him. "So many merits."

He engaged his com. "What do you need, Firoh?"

"Just wanted you to know we're within hailing distance of the Plushier Space Station."

"So soon?"

"I caught a solar wind. Never seen anything like it, but after the island, I embraced it. We should make port within an horus."

"Is an horus enough?" he whispered in my ear. "Or should I ask him to make some loops around the orbiting moon before making port?"

"Hmm." I scrunched my face, pretending I needed time to think about this. "An horus will never be enough," I said softly, so Firoh wouldn't overhear. "But we can make do. If you're good."

"Take us to the space station," he told Firoh. "Let me know when we've made port."

"Very well, boss." Firoh ended the call.

Matis tugged me closer. "Time to show you how good I can truly be, mate."

And he did.

CHAPTER FORTY
TATUM
EPILOGUE

One lunar cycle later.

"Are you sure you want to buy them?" I asked Matis.

Leaning against the fence in Kreel and Cora's backyard, I gazed skeptically at the tiny culair pups playing near their enormous parents. I wasn't too worried about the cuties. As for their parents? Let's just say I had a healthy respect for enormous beasts.

"I'm very sure," Matis said. "They're just what we need. Two should do it, unless you think we should buy four."

Four? I barely held back my wince.

Pets were my thing. Even Snuggles didn't appear frightened of them. He kept leaping toward them, then scampering away with his tail in the air, hoping they'd give chase. So far, they were too busy playing amongst themselves to pay any attention to him.

Their parents, however, appeared to be the stuff of nightmares. With their glowing red eyes, they resembled dragons straight from an Earth fairytale. The only difference I could discern was their lack of wings. I guess it was good they couldn't fly; otherwise, they'd swoop down and snatch up prey—and I suspected we'd be their first victims.

Smoke coiled from their snouts. Could they shoot fire? I didn't want to find out.

"They're gorgeous, don't you think?" Matis said with complete joy.

"*I* think so," Mom said from beside me.

"Me too," Firoh said. He stood on the other side of Mom.

After leaving Firoh on the Plushier Space Station where he would collect his sons and take them home, we'd flown to Earth.

Matis had saved most of his wages through the yaros, and he'd easily paid for Mom's treatment. She was completely cured and told us she couldn't wait to travel into the stars. Other than living with us at the colony, she said she was contemplating getting her own small ship and doing some exploring. I'd seen her flirting with one of the other colonists, and it thrilled me to see her happy and healthy.

We'd recently settled in the same colony as Kreel and

Cora, and they were helping us build our new home. Mom's place would be completed after that. She wanted to live near us, but she needed her own space.

I'd be horribly embarrassed if she walked in on Matis riding me hard while calling me a good girl.

As for Firoh, he'd decided to relocate here with his two younglings. They'd arrived not long after us, and Firoh said he hoped he'd soon be able to hire a nanny to help him raise them. He was working with the Interstellar Employment Agency to find one.

"Once you train them, they will be just what you need to till your fields and pull your wagon into town," Kreel said from the other side of Matis.

Firoh nodded. The three guys were about the same height and build, though Kreel was an orc, not an ogre, and Firoh was a Chullod warrior. There were other distinctive differences between them. Both Firoh and Kreel had a tail and horns, as did Kreel's toddler son, Hrall, something uncommon in ogres.

Kreel's mate, Cora, stood with him, holding their son on her hip. Her long blonde hair streamed out behind her in the breeze, and the tufts dancing on Hrall's head suggested he would have hair the same color as hers, though his skin color was pure orc like his dad.

If me and Matis had a child, something we hadn't talked about yet, what would they look like? I kind of hoped they had Matis's copper skin, though I was partial to my own hair color.

"I think two culairs will do for now," I said. Maybe it

wouldn't be bad. If we raised them with loving care, they wouldn't turn their fire our way, would they?

"Two it is," Matis said, his arm going around my back. "You pick out which ones we should take."

"Are you sure?" I said. "You'll be working with them more than me."

"Of course."

"Alright." I slipped between the rails of the fence, glancing Kreel's way. "It's okay to go near them?"

"Yes, yes," he said, leaping over the rail with one bound. He landed solidly beside me.

Cora put Hrall down and he crawled beneath the lowest rail, aiming for the culair babies. She watched him, a big grin on her face.

If she wasn't afraid of the huge parents, maybe I shouldn't be either.

Firoh remained on the other side of the fence. He'd mentioned letting his youngling sons help pick out his own culairs once they'd settled.

I moved slowly across the grass. Snuggles galloped over to sashay beside me, his tail swishing back and forth through the air.

"What do you think, little guy?" I asked him.

He looked up at me and started to purr.

The crystal I now wore strung on a chain around my neck started humming, a lilting tune that soothed my jittery nerves. I still couldn't get over it bonding with me.

I didn't know what it might have in store for me, but I was eager to find out.

"Only eight pups in this group," Kreel said, waving to the culair young as he walked beside me. Hrall kept up, crawling right behind him while making cute smacking sounds with his lips.

Matis leapt over the fence, joining us. He scooped up Snuggles and dropped the creature on his shoulder, then took my hand.

"Is it better to pick males or females?" I asked, checking the pups out. They were incredibly cute; there was no denying that.

"Either," Kreel said.

When I got near enough to touch, I kept a wide eye on their parents, but the creatures grazed, ignoring how close we were to their young.

As I tiptoed even closer, Matis hung back with Kreel, who hefted Hrall and placed the youngling on his shoulder. Hrall latched onto one of Kreel's horns and rocked, kicking his legs and squealing.

My crystal kept singing, and the lovely tune calmed me. When I could reach out and touch the pups, I sat on the ground.

They immediately swarmed me, climbing all over me and licking my face like puppies do back on Earth. In no time, I was rolling around with them, rubbing bellies and scratching behind their ears. My laughter rang in the air, as did Mom's. She shouted encouragement, and nothing made me happier than seeing her smile. Her cough was gone, and her face gleamed with good health.

Matis dropped beside me and helped me sit up,

plucking three of the pups off me so I could remain upright.

"What's it going to be, mate?" he asked me, his arm around my back. Leaning over, he kissed the top of my head. "Pick."

I grinned up at him, so grateful to have this male in my life. Where would I be without him? "I love you, Matis."

"And I love you, Tatum. But the pups?"

"Ah, the pups," I said, studying them. "Why don't we take them all?"

Would you like to read a Bonus Scene
from Pirating the Alien?
Sign up for my newsletter
& it's yours!

Want a FREE book?
Escorting the Alien, a complete
romance with a HEA & part of the
Beastly Alien Boss world,
is yours free when you
Sign Up for My Newsletter!

If you'd like to read Cora & Kreel's story,
pick up Nailing the Alien

For Charlie (Matis's sister) & Shaede's story,
get Handcuffing the Alien

And for a peek at Molly & Firoh's romance,
grab Schooling the Alien
Scroll ahead for the first chapter . . .

ABOUT THE AUTHOR

Ava Ross is a two-time *USA Today* Bestselling author of numerous titles. She fell for men with unusual features when she first watched Star Wars, where alien creatures have gone mainstream. She lives in New England with her husband (who is sadly not an alien, though he is still cute in his own way), her kids, and a few assorted pets.

SERIES BY AVA

Mail-Order Brides of Crakair

Brides of Driegon

Fated Mates of the Ferlaern Warriors

Fated Mates of the Xilan Warriors

Holiday with a Cu'zod Warrior

Galaxy Games

Alien Warrior Abandoned

Beastly Alien Boss

Bride of the Fae

A Sci-Fi Holiday Tail

Monsterville, USA

Monster on Board
(co-written with Alana Khan)

You can find Ava's books on Amazon.

SCHOOLING THE ALIEN

**Do I dare give my broken heart to
an alien as wounded as me?**

When I took a nanny job in a distant colony, caring for two young boys who recently lost their mother, I expected I'd grow to love them. Having experienced loss myself, I knew how hard it was to heal. What I didn't expect was to fall for their father, a big, burly alien with scars on his body that mirrors those in my soul.

Between teaching the boys and bringing fun back into their lives, I get to know Firoh, a guy I sense needs love as much as me. It isn't long before I can see myself living in this alien colony forever, as long as I can be with Firoh and his sons.

But when the boys' past threatens everything Firoh and I are building together, we'll have to expose our hearts to each other to fight off the threat.

Schooling the Alien is Book 8 and the final book in the Beastly Alien Boss Series. Each book is standalone and loosely connected. They can be read in any order. Expect strong women and heroes who will do anything to be with their fated mates.

Trigger: the loss of a child in the main character's history, prior to the start of the book, and Firoh's sons have lost their mother. Readers do not experience this with the characters, though they refer to it and mourn.

Get Schooling the Alien Now!

CHAPTER 1
MOLLY

Once my divorce was final, I packed my things. I stood in the front hall afterward, realizing how few possessions I had compared to Tyler. Only three boxes after ten years of marriage.

Plus one teardrop blue stone I wore strung on a simple chain about my neck, all I had left of the baby I'd lost before I could deliver her a year ago.

"I'll help you put them in your vehicle," Tyler said, his face stoic as always. I imagined it would loosen up after I'd left.

He left Bridgette's side, striding to the front door.

I did my best not to notice her softly bulging belly. He'd barely waited six months after I lost our daughter before planting a new child in someone else.

"I can handle it," I said.

Since I had no place to go, he'd lived with Bridgette until I could "get my feet under me". Now that the divorce was final, however, I had to move out. The house and everything inside it legally belonged to my wealthy ex. Per our prenup, I got a small stipend that would be just enough to rent an apartment, though not enough to eat or buy myself a new pair of shoes.

It was okay. I could get a job.

Lifting a box, I propped it on my hip, then grabbed my bag of clothing. "You can get the door for me, Tyler. Maybe place the other boxes out on the stoop? I'll put these inside my hover car," mine being a generous way to describe the rental, "Then come back for the other two."

"Don't be like that," he snapped. "I'll take them to your hovercar."

So generous.

Bridgette released a shrill laugh, quickly cutting it off with a hand slapped over her mouth.

In the past, I would've strode right up to him, poked him in the chest, and told him I could be any way I pleased. Now, I just gave him one of those looks that made him squirm. I didn't have much else I could use to defend myself.

Outside, I shivered in the chilly winter air, taking care on the walk not to slip.

Tyler followed me with the final boxes stacked in his arms, leaving Bridgette inside the house. He opened the trunk of the small hovercar and lowered my few possessions inside. "What do you plan to do?"

"You know me. I always bounce back. I've got a new job lined up, and I'll start that soon."

I'll forget I was ever with you, I didn't add. Over the past six months, I'd already done most of the work of pushing him out of my heart and my life. I mourned the loss of our daughter more than I did our marriage.

"Hey, I'm glad to hear that," he said with forced cheer. "I'm sure you'll do fine."

He didn't give a damn what I did or how I felt now. He'd moved on.

It was time I did the same.

I placed the final box in the trunk and shut it, striding to the driver's side door. "See you around."

"Yeah." He lifted his hand in a half-hearted wave. I was sure his mind was already back inside, with Bridgette.

After engaging the engine, the craft lifted off the ground. I programmed it to take me to my new apartment.

I didn't look back as the vehicle took the main road into the city. Other hovercars flew on either side of me, everyone having someplace to go but me.

One problem loomed in my future.

I'd lied. I had no job, no new life waiting for me. Just a ratty apartment and three food packs to create about nine meals in the apartment's tiny synthesizer. If I was lucky, I could stretch the credits in my bank account until I got my next alimony check. I had no other choice, now did I?

"What should I do?" I asked the air around me as the hovercar zipped across town, taking me to the seedier side, the only place where I could afford a rental. Apartment was being generous, since it was one room. But it furnished with a narrow bed, a small kitchen table and stool, plus a dingy sofa, so I couldn't complain.

The teardrop stone I wore on a chain around my neck shifted across my skin. I'd bought it after my loss and worn it all the time since.

I wrapped my fingers around it. Clung to it, actually, the only thing I valued above all else. At least Tyler hadn't suggested I leave it behind. I would've fought him on that one.

Straightening, my gaze focused on a sign mounted above the door of the building coming up on my right.

Intergalactic Employment Agency.

I could swear the stone grew warmer, but things like that just didn't happen.

"Maybe I should find a job in outer space. Leave Earth and never return. What do you think about that?" I stroked the stone, feeling closer to my daughter than I had for months.

Halting the ship's program, I engaged the hovercar's landing sequence. The craft dropped down onto the pavement, and I got out, waiting while aliens of all sizes and shapes passed me on the walkway.

"This is stupid," I whispered, studying the sign as if it would tell me what to do. Jobs were scarce in the city for those who'd gone from high school straight into marriage.

After pinching my eyes closed, I opened them again. I locked the hovercar and wove around people and up to the front door. I sucked in a breath and released it before opening the door and stepping inside.

"Welcome to the Intergalactic Employment Agency," a robot called out from the back of the bright room. With a rhythmic whir and a bang-bang-bang of its steps, the robot rolled toward me on plexi tracks, extending its metal hand. "How can I help you today?"

"I'm looking for a job," I said, though it must be obvious. Why else come here? "Something off-world?"

"Of course," the robot said, tilting its head to the dash floating nearby. "Are you sure?"

I frowned. "Why wouldn't I be?"

"Lazy days and sleepless nights are no way to proceed through life."

"Excuse me?"

The robot shuddered. Its glowing yellow eyes flashed a few times before solidifying, pointed my way. "I do apologize. My programming has been faulty lately. I'm due for reboot soon. Would you care to come back later, once it's finished?"

"Are you saying you won't be able to help me find a job?" Why open the business this dia if the device wasn't functioning correctly?

"I'm fully capable of that. Just . . . please expect occasional glitches."

"Okay." Maybe this was a mistake. I should go to my apartment, unpack my boxes, and then hit the streets, looking for a job near where I lived. Before marrying Tyler, I'd worked in a care facility in the breaks between school sessions. Skills like that never faded. They must have openings.

"Before we proceed," the robot said. "I will need your name and com information."

I lifted my wrist com for scanning.

"I see your employment is limited," the robot said, its voice lacking inflection.

"I'm recently divorced," I said. "I'm starting a new life. My ex didn't want me working while we were married." Or doing much of anything else but cater to him, but I didn't need to share that with everyone I ran into.

"Singing strange melodies of trees," the robot said.

Doubts shot through my mind, but I persisted. I needed a job; this was an employment agency.

"Again, I apologize," the robot said, its gears grinding as it rolled behind the plexi-topped counter, the dash hovering beside it. "I can offer you three positions. First, a Xilan is looking for someone to provide services during his slaking."

"What's a Xilan and what's a slaking?"

The robot leveled me a long look with its glowing white eyes. "You would perform sexually for a one-week period while the Xilan male is in heat."

"I have nothing against sex workers, but I don't believe that's the right position for me. What else do you have?"

"Flights of fancy result in nine lives."

"Yeah, sure." My laugh burst out, loosening my heavy emotions. If nothing else, this was entertaining. It wasn't a complete waste of time even if the robot couldn't come up with anything for me.

"The second position is for a tour guide."

That might work. "Tour guide for what type of operation?"

"There is a training period before you begin, of course."

"I'm sure." I leaned on the top of the counter, eager. "What kind of tours?"

"Primarily on an asteroid cluster. The owner is seeking someone to take adventurers deep below the surface, into the cave systems. You would, of course, have to take the necessary precautions while there."

I straightened, not so eager any longer. "I assume I'll wear equipment?"

"If you did not, you would not only float off the asteroid, you would die within three nanoseconds. Oxygen would be limited to the suit wearer."

"I'm not much of an adventurer." And I enjoyed breathing.

"One cannot be picky when one has no work experience."

Despite the robot's lack of inflection, I sensed it mocked me.

"Anything else?" I asked, my heart sinking. Why had I bothered to come here?

"Erratic words falling from the sky can hit harder than a fist." The robot shuddered before speaking again. "The last position would require you to travel to a new colony on Merth 4X7."

"Where is Merth 4X7?"

"A planet in the Thrushalon Sector," the robot said.

"Tell me more about this colony and planet." The last thing I wanted to do was accept a job in an icy wasteland —or on an oxygen-deprived asteroid, for that matter.

"Merth 4X7 is located in the Sebula Quadrant. It's an agricultural planet with three colonies, primarily growing hemp. Indigenous populations, none. Settlers, three thousand eighty-nine, most live in the other colonies, not the one with this opening. Water, potable. Air, breathable. Gravity is approximate to this planet. Merth 4X7 is twenty-seven-point-two light years from Earth. You would need to travel in suspension."

Most jobs required that when a person traveled off-world. "Would I need to wear special equipment while I worked there?"

"Of course not," the robot said. "Lizard aliens often kill their prey."

Truly, they needed to reboot this device soon.

"What kind of job would I perform there?" I asked.

"The male hiring someone wants a three yaro commitment."

"Why so long?" Not that I was opposed to taking a long-term position. It wasn't like I had much else on my agenda.

"The position pays quite well." The robot named a salary that, after three yaros, would ensure I could take care of myself for a long time once I returned to Earth. That would give me time to get an education so I could find a job that would support me for the rest of my life.

"What would I do?" I asked, figuring there had to be a trick.

"The male is looking for someone to care for his twin younglings."

My heart clenched at the thought. "Why does he need help?"

The robot leaned over the dash, reading. "I am not at liberty to share those details."

Figured that. It was confidential. "How old are they?"

"Six-yaros-old."

I didn't know what to do. Could I care for someone else's children so soon after losing my own? Stroking my pendant, I sighed.

I could be imagining it, but I swore the teardrop stone hummed.

"I'll take the job," I said.

"Very well. Your com, please."

I lifted my wrist, and the robot scanned the device, programming it and his dash with the necessary information.

"Taste is subjective, don't you think?" the robot asked, its eyes flashing again. "My fuel is electricity."

"I assumed so." I cringed, wondering if this was the biggest mistake of my life. No, that would be marrying Tyler. This would be an . . . adventure. "When can I leave?"

"Now or tomorrow."

"So soon?"

"The male Chullod has sought a caregiver for six lunar cycles."

Nothing was keeping me here. If I left right away, I

wouldn't need to watch Bridgette's belly grow bigger, a reminder of what I'd lost.

"If I say now," I said. "Could you arrange storage for my possessions? They're in the rented hovercar parked on the curb outside."

"I believe the position will allow for that," the robot said.

"Then now it is."

A transport pod dropped down into a chute behind the robot, landing on the floor with a solid thud. The front panel opened.

I waved to the street. "Let me grab my bag, and I'll be ready to go."

The robot dipped its head forward. "Bird feathers are often slippery."

I paused with my fingers on the front door. "Can you guarantee you won't mess up and send me to the wrong destination."

The robot huffed. "The pod is programmed to take you to the position on Merth 4X7."

"Alright." Nothing to lose, right? It was an adventure, something I could share with my friends one day—once I had friends, something else Tyler had discouraged.

I hated it here. Everything reminded me of what I'd lost, that I essentially had no future.

Better to trust fate to handle this for me.

My bag in hand, I stepped inside the pod. The lid sealed, and gas flooded the chamber.

The last thing I saw was the robot peering into the pod. "One last thing."

"What?" My head spun, and the world was losing focus.

"Every westalon is a trite—"

My vision wavered, and I gave into the lull of stasis. Whatever the robot said was lost to me forever.

I woke to the lid of my pod opening.

Sitting up, I peered around at a lush, lavender lawn with a forest beyond, peppered with vegetation from every color in the rainbow.

"A pod, a pod," a young voice shouted.

Two alien children, one with purple skin and silver hair, the other more human-appearing and with dark hair, clung to the side of my travel pod.

One smiled. The other scowled.

The scowling one pointed a laser gun at my head. "Kill her!"

Get Schooling the Alien NOW!